The Firefighter & The Amish Widow

Hannah Winstone

Published by Trellis Publishing, 2021.

THE FIREFIGHTER & THE AMISH WIDOW

First edition. July 12, 2021.

Copyright © 2021 Hannah Winstone.

ISBN: 979-8223510390

Written by Hannah Winstone.

THE FIREFIGHTER & THE AMISH WIDOW

1

HANNAH WINSTONE

Billy didn't spend much time in the small Amish community - he wasn't Amish himself, didn't have any family - but he loved how everyone was so friendly, so willing to help, and treated him like he was one of them. The fact that he was one of the local firemen from the next town over likely helped; he had rescued a lot of these people over the years.

A young man with a child smiled as he passed, and Billy offered a cheerful wave. "Good morning." He didn't recognise the man's round face or dark blue eyes, so he didn't stop to chat. He had places to be after all; namely the bakery that made those fantastic apple pies. He crossed the street, saving a glance toward his favourite butcher's shop - and then stumbled backward as something tiny and soft careened into his legs.

A...kid?

Billy blinked stupidly, lips parted even though no words came out. The girl couldn't have been older than eight or nine, with big blue eyes and a shock of strawberry blonde hair.

"Sorry mister!" The girl beamed, bouncing on her heels as she skipped backwards.

A frown graced his features, eyes darting up. "Where's your parents?"

"Oh, Mum's just coming-"

A young woman appeared from around the corner, her grey eyes wide as she honed in on Billy and the girl. "Hannah!" she shouted, hurrying over to take the girl - Hannah - by the hand. "What did I tell you about running off? Are you all right?" Then, her slender face turned to Billy she asked, "she didn't bother you, I hope?"

No reply came. He *knew* her face, couldn't ever forget it. Sharp cheekbones and thin, angular eyebrows. Wide grey-blue eyes like a stormy sky. All framed by thick, wavy blonde hair messily tied in a half-bun.

"Greta?"

She blinked - and then realisation dawned. The corner of her lips dimpled as she *beamed,* a laugh bubbling up in her throat. "Billy? Billy Strickland?" She looked so *young* when she smiled at him, like it had only been a handful of months since they last spoke. Not the eight years it had really been. "I didn't recognise you! The beard is new. So is the ear piercing."

"Midlife crisis," he admitted with a laugh. He was only thirty-two, but it had been an impulsive decision nonetheless. "How are you doing, Greta?"

"Wonderful, thanks to you. If you hadn't helped me all those years ago, who know where I would be now."

He hadn't done much - but he would still remember that day forever. It had been an overcast evening on his way home from work; there had been a wagon on the country road, a woman lying in the field. Her husband hovered over her as she let out a strangled cry - and Billy had rushed to them, panic swelling in his chest. Greta had been pregnant, and that evening Billy had helped her give birth. To Hannah, he supposed.

Greta's sunshine smile broke him from his thoughts. "How have you been?" she asked - and then stepped to the side as a scowling man walked past. "Eight years. Lots must have changed?"

They had only met once, but they fell into step together like old friends. Billy wasn't even sure where they were going, but he let Greta lead him. "Oh, I suppose things *have* changed. I'm still a firefighter - I don't think I could ever give that up - but I've moved house. I became an uncle last year; my youngest sister had her first kid. And, uh, I'm living with someone."

"Are you *married?*" Hannah piped up. Her enormous eyes made her look like a baby deer. Or an owl.

Greta huffed, but was hiding a smile behind her hand. "You don't ask people those things, love."

Yet he laughed easily. "No, not yet. Holly... well, she likes to have things her own way. And that means my proposal will have to be *perfect.*" Although to be truthful, Billy wasn't sure he wanted to marry Holly. She was fun, and beautiful, and had her life together in a way he could only dream. But... well, there were problems too. Shaking his head, Billy changed the subject. "What about you, Greta? How's your marriage treating you."

Her steps faltered, a sigh hissing from between her lips. Her very *full,* rosy lips. "Mark and I divorced six years ago." Her eyes darted around the street as if afraid someone might hear her. Right, divorce wasn't exactly accepted here. Biting down on her lip she leaned closer to murmur, "Mark was... well, he wasn't as perfect as he made himself seem; I ended it before he could get violent."

Billy had to suppress a shudder. *Violent?* All those years ago, Mark had seemed like the model husband. Someone worried about his wife and desperate to see her safe. He never could have foreseen something like this - but wasn't that the point? He didn't know either him nor Greta.

"I don't want to talk about it," Greta said before Billy could even ask. Folding her arms, she looked down to Hannah - who either wasn't listening or didn't seem to care. Kids bounced back from trauma far quicker than adults. Billy's line of work taught him so. "Look," Greta continued with a scowl, "I have to go. I'm so busy, especially since Hannah isn't old enough to leave in the house."

"Right." Disappointment settled in his chest; disappointment he couldn't quite place.

Her next comment lifted his spirits, though. "Are you free Monday? I could use the company..."

"I'd love to." He answered too quickly, too *eagerly,* but he didn't have it in him to care. He offered her a grin and said, "Monday is perfect. Say, two-ish?"

"I'll meet you at Ainsel's bakery?"

It was as if she had read his mind. "Great. See you then." Billy couldn't figure out why his heart was so jittery, or why he couldn't stop grinning - but as they said their goodbyes, it was impossible to ignore the fact it was because of *her*.

———————————

The thought of seeing Greta again caused a spark of excitement in Billy's chest Monday afternoon. It shouldn't have, because it was just lunch between two sort-of friends who wanted to catch up. In fact, Greta was little more than an acquaintance. It didn't stop him from feeling giddy though, but he tried not to think too much about *why* that was.

Unfortunately for him, Holly didn't feel so enthusiastic. When he slipped into the kitchen for a glass of water, there she was. Hands on hips, green eyes narrowed into a scowl. It was her default expression really, but it never failed to make Billy wince. "Where are you going in such a rush?"

"I told you this morning; out with a friend."

"A friend? You mean that *sweet* Amish woman with the kid?"

Right. He should have seen this coming. Running a hand through his thick blond hair, Billy sighed. "Yes, with Greta."

If it was even possible, Holly's eyes narrowed further. Holly was the picture of a young suburban woman; neatly kept dark hair, tanned skin and long legs, wrapped up in a simple summer dress and cardigan. Yet that scowl was more menacing than anything a man like Billy could pull off.

"Just for an hour or two," he promised, "and you'll be at work anyway."

"Exactly. I'll be slaving away in that damn office while you flounce off with some *woman*. You're not going, William."

Ah, she was bringing out his full name now. He hated to admit how it made his heart clench with anxiety, how he had to fight not to snap at her. Here they were arguing over the same thing they'd argued over a hundred times before; his social life. As soon as he wanted to spend time with another woman? This happened.

Making his way to the sink, Billy pointedly avoided her gaze. He took his time pouring a drink, then sipped on it slowly as he turned around. "Holly," he started, punctuating each syllable, "we're going out for coffee and cake. Besides that she's *Amish,* she wouldn't want anything even if I did."

"So you admit you *do* want something with her?"

"That isn't - what?"

She was *really* glaring now, her thick pencilled brows forming a harsh line above her eyes. She huffed out a breath, threw her hands in the air, and stormed out of the room. The *click* of heels followed her all the way into the hall.

Billy hesitated for a moment, cheeks burning in frustration, before swearing quietly and jogging after her. He managed to catch her at the bottom of the stairs, where she had paused to glare at a photograph of the two of them on the side table. "Holly, *listen.*" He was tired of making excuses, of defending himself for doing perfectly normal things, but the sight of her so angry made his stomach curl. "I'll be two hours, tops. We only want to catch up; it's been eight years after all-"

"You met this girl what, once? So why do you care so much about a *catch up* anyway? Am I not enough?"

Anger bubbled up inside of him. A frustrated sigh rose in his throat but Billy swallowed it down. "People are allowed to have friends, Holly. *I'm* allowed to. This paranoia of yours is exactly that, and it isn't my fault that you insist on seeing things that aren't there."

She whirled on him then, slender finger jabbing into his chest with a scowl that could send the even scariest person running. "Fine. Do what you want, I don't care. But I'm your *girlfriend,* and you should be prioritising me. Not some stupid Amish girl you don't even know." She shoved past him, thin shoulder digging into his broader one, before marching back across the hall and out the back door. Billy lost sight of her once she stormed away from the porch, and he imagined her cursing him out the entire way.

That went about as well as expected. Worse, even, which was quite an achievement considering Holly was known for these awful outbursts. She had been like this for the entire two years they had been together; at first, Billy had put it down to the anxiety of a new relationship, to paranoia from previous romance gone wrong. Now, he knew it for what it was; an attempt to control him.

Well, too bad for Holly. His blood was still rushing through his ears, but at least the rapid thud of his heart had calmed. He wasn't going to let her get the better of him; he was going to enjoy his afternoon with Greta, enjoy the delicious food served at Ainsel's bakery, and Holly wasn't going to get in the way of that.

Did it make him sound spiteful? Maybe. Uncaring? Probably. Yet he couldn't quite bring himself to care, especially after not that mess of an argument. She needed time to cool off, that was all, and then they'd make up.

Billy didn't give himself a chance to think about it. Within minutes he was throwing on his coat - not that the bright summer sun required one - and locking the front door behind himself. He had to take the bus, since the little Amish town didn't have anywhere to park his enormous four-by-four, but the quiet walk to the bus stop helped to clear his mind.

By the time he reached the bakery, inhaling the sweet smell of pastries and pie, he had almost forgotten about his foul start to the afternoon. Then he saw Greta's smiling face from inside, pushed open the door, and the last of his mad mood was forgotten entirely.

Hannah was there too, her smile perking as she caught sight of him. She was exactly like her mother; strawberry blonde hair tied in two little plaits, greyish blue eyes like a stormy sea, fair skin and a narrow jaw. He should have seen the resemblance right away, but it wasn't until

Greta that he thought about it. Thankfully, she didn't look too much like her father.

Greta ushered him over with a grin. There weren't many tables, as most customers bought their sweets to take home, but there was a collection of dainty tables and chairs near the window. Greta stood as he neared, arms reaching to envelop him in a hug. She was so warm and soft, smelled faintly of the pastries surrounding them - but also something distinctly *Greta*.

He shouldn't hug her like this, but Billy didn't care. Instead he wrapped his arms around her tiny waist and buried his face in her hair. "What's the welcome for?" he murmured, fighting a laugh. And the urge to tug her closer.

Greta broke the embrace first, laughter dancing in her eyes. "I think it's only fair, given how long it's been," she replied with a beaming smile, "I hope you don't mind that I brought Hannah. She *should* be in school, but she begged me to let her see you again..."

He glanced down to the young girl, who was sipping on a glass of fresh juice. "School is boring," she replied with a nod, "I like this better."

Honestly, Billy figured she just wanted a free day and cake, but his heart warmed at the thought she wanted to see *him*. He'd never been good with kids, had never wanted any of his own - but as Hannah's sweet face peered up at him, he realised he must have done *something* right for Hannah to like him.

As they settled back down, Billy took a moment to survey the cakes. Greta peered over his shoulder to recommend the carrot cake, her breath tickling the shell of his ear. Did she realise how close she was? So close he could hear every breath, feel every beat of her heart. Had she scooted her chair forward too, just to get closer?

It's all perfectly innocent, he told himself, *she's not interested in you.* Yet a small voice in the back of his head argued, *Holly wouldn't think so, if she saw this.* Holly wasn't here, though - Greta was. So he shoved those negative thoughts somewhere deep down, let an easy smile spread across his lips, and ordered a slice of carrot cake.

"I know we're not supposed to eat a lot of desserts," Greta mused as she lifted her fork, "I mean, I don't eat an *unhealthy* amount, but more than I should. Rhubarb pie is my biggest weakness. I suppose that's why I love this place so much."

"I've been going here since the beginning," Billy admitted with a laugh, "ever since it opened up what, four years ago?"

Greta's eyes sparkled, lips curving into a beautiful smile. "You love it here too do you? I'm glad; it *is* my bakery after all."

Billy gaped. It was *what?*

For a moment he thought he might have heard wrong - but then Hannah giggled, big eyes wide. "Daddy left us lots of money, enough to start a bakery!"

"It was about the only good thing he did for us, before he left." Greta's smile faltered; but then it was back, radiant as ever. "Anyway, I've always dreamed of owning a bakery, so I did."

"But I've never seen you here," Billy fumbled, staring down at one perfect slice of carrot cake. Even the icing was flawless, piped expertly. "Wouldn't I have ran into you over the years?"

Greta swept a loose strand of hair behind her ear, head tilted as she gazed at him in amusement. "I own the place, but I don't have a front facing role. I work in the back as one of the bakers."

Oh. *Oh!* How often had Billy eaten her cake and never known? Was this slice of cake hers too? His cheeks flushed - and he didn't know why, because it didn't matter, but all of a sudden his entire face was burning.

Greta smirked, nudging Hannah with a knowing smile. "He's cute when he's flustered, isn't he?"

Hannah grinned, eyes dancing between Billy and her mother.

"You're teasing," he stated.

"Only because you make it so easy."

Brow quirked, Billy went back to his cake. It was the perfect contrast of sweet and savoury, dense but not too heavy, and the cream cheese icing was *exactly* how he always liked it. Now he knew why Greta gave such a good recommendation. The thought brought a smile to his lips.

"So what about you?" Greta asked as she started on her pie, "I divorced my husband and started a bakery. What about *you?*"

Ah. The worst part about catching up - you were expected to talk about yourself, too. Wincing, he replied, "I told you I have a girlfriend. We moved in together last year."

"The girlfriend you don't want to marry!" Hannah piped up. Billy flushed, Greta scowled, but she just kept on smiling.

"*Hannah,*" Greta hissed, "don't say things like that-"

"You should marry Mother instead!"

Greta paled, and although her lips parted she didn't say a word.

Hannah, in all her youthful ignorance, didn't seem to realise she had said anything wrong.

"I'm sorry," Greta murmured, "she doesn't mean it, you know, it's just silly things children say-"

"Don't worry about it," Billy reassured. He just hoped his tanned skin hid the worst of his horrible flushing. He doubted his long hair would hide the pink tint of his ears, though.

They carried on after that, as if nothing had happened. They slipped back into easy chatter with little difficulty, but Hannah's words never quite left his mind. He wasn't going to marry Greta, of course, but it had opened up a part of him he hadn't allowed himself to think about.

Did he love Greta? No, they hardly knew each other. That didn't stop him from thinking, from wondering what it would be like to be with her.

He barely knew her, sure, but already he was falling for her anyway.

————————————

He knew the day would come. The day when Holly went too far, or he snapped, or something else came along and he just didn't want this any more. He just never imagined *he* would be the one breaking up with *her.*

Holly's seafoam eyes blinked at him from across the kitchen table, her hand folded neatly on her lap. She was unusually calm despite the hard set of her jaw and sloping scowl of her eyebrows. "What did you want to talk about, honey?"

She knew. The words popped into his mind completely of their own accord, and instantly Billy knew it was true. Holly already knew why he had sat her down, why he had been so nervous the entire morning. Somehow, either because of his own inability to hold secrets or through deduction, she knew what he was going to say.

Yet still he tried to let her down kindly. With a soft sigh, he tried to ignore the thundering of his heart. "Holly, you know I love you right?"

"I'd certainly hope so." She cracked a smile. Forced.

"I've loved you since we first met, and I still do, but I don't... I don't think I can keep doing this. *Us.*" A heavy breath, stomach clenching. Yet he forced himself to continue. He *needed* to do this, even if it was so impossibly difficult he wanted to be sick. "You've changed, Holly. I mean everyone does - I have too - but over the years you've just gotten more and more controlling and I don't know *why-*"

"I'm not controlling," she snapped, "you just insist on doing things I don't like."

"You don't like when I do *anything,* and that's kind of the point."

Holly glared. She was pretty even as she stared daggers at him, her face scrunching in such a way she somehow still looked like an angel. Too bad Billy knew the truth, had known it far longer than he wanted to admit. "Is this about that Amish woman?" she demanded, arms folded across her chest, "Grace or Gemma or whatever."

"Greta."

"Oh, who *cares* what her name is! This all started when you bumped into her. Are you in love with her, Billy? You've found someone nicer and prettier so you're getting rid of me?"

What? Did she really think he was that shallow? Yes, he liked Greta - and maybe, if he was completely honest, he had the potential to love her. This wasn't about her though - this was about him and Holly, and how Greta had made him realise that *this* wasn't a relationship. Not a real one. Not a healthy one. It was just two people going through the motions - and not even doing it well.

What he felt when he was with Greta? He had never felt like that around Holly. *Never.* Perhaps it was cruel to say, but that didn't make it any less true.

Lips pursed, eyes narrowed, Holly stared him down. She wasn't going to accept this without a fight, and Billy knew it.

"I'm sorry, but this was a long time coming. You have to see that."

"I don't see anything except an *asshole.* You love Greta, and she's the only reason you're even doing this. You'd never have the courage otherwise."

"That isn't *fair-*"

"Oh, and it *is* fair for you to swan off with some Amish chick and leave me behind?"

That wasn't what he was doing. Greta was only a tiny fraction of what was wrong with all of this - she hadn't done anything except let him see the truth. Maybe Holly was right; maybe he *wouldn't* have done anything if it wasn't for Greta. That didn't mean there weren't problems, it just meant he had never seen them before.

"Holly please, there's no need to-"

She wasn't listening any more. Launching to her feet, the chair skittering backward, she was already leaving. That was her way; leave when things went wrong. Avoid. Pretend everything was fine until she *snapped.*

Billy leapt to his feet, sprinting across the kitchen. He caught her by the wrist, spinning to block the doorway before she could storm all the way outside. "Come on, can't we just talk about this?"

"What's to talk about?" she snapped, wrenching her wrist from his grasp. She rubbed it as if he had *hurt her,* although it had been a ghost of a touch. Holly edged to the side, trying to squeeze past - but Billy's broad shoulders took up every inch of the doorway. "Just let me past!"

"Not until we-"

"I'm not discussing *anything* with you. We've broken up, haven't we? I don't owe you anything; not even a conversation."

"Seriously? How *petty-*"

"Oh, I can be pettier." She was smaller than him, barely reaching his chin, but her glare sent a shiver down his spine. "That pretty Amish girl of yours? You'd better watch her, because I'm not going to make things easy for her. Or you."

A threat? His eyes narrowed, hands clenching by his side. "You don't mean that-"

"Oh I do. I'm going to make sure *everyone* knows how you've betrayed me."

Lips parted to reply - but he never had the chance. Holly shoved past with enough force to send him stumbling, catching him off guard at just the right time to stalk past. She didn't look back, didn't so much as acknowledge him as she grabbed her jacket. Seconds later the door slammed shut behind her.

Billy watched from the kitchen window as she marched down the driveway. Where was she going? Better yet, what was going to happen now? He knew where he would go - his mother's. Just for a few days, until Holly cooled down enough to talk properly. Until she got her stuff together and moved out.

But what about Greta?

———————————————

Over the weeks, things began to die down. Holly moved out with little fuss, her threats empty and without venom. The air cleared, after that - whatever heavy feelings that were lingering left along with her.

Of course, he told Greta everything. Well, almost everything. He left out the part about it being, in a way, about *her.* Because despite the way he denied it, it *was* true. Holly had been right; he was in love with Greta.

No, he hadn't mentioned it; but today, as he waited anxiously by the park gates, he was going to. A breeze rustled past, but the sky overhead blazed hot yellow. Billy was beginning to sweat, hands turning clammy, and it wasn't just because of the sun.

Then he spotted her. Greta. Her beautiful hair was tied in a braid, a few strands pulled loose by the breeze. She tucked them behind her ear as she spotted him, face breaking into a smile. "Billy! Good morning." She all but fell into his arms, all soft curves and softer hair. It was becoming a habit for her; the easy touches, the embraces.

He enjoyed it more than he probably should.

"How are you?" Greta asked, falling into step beside him. "You asked me here in such a hurry, I thought something was wrong!"

It *was* true. He had appeared by her door that morning, annoyed by her pack of phone but eager for any excuse to see her face to face. He'd all but demanded she see him later, so sure of himself. That confidence had only lasted until Greta agreed. Biting down on his lip, Billy let his gaze cast across the park. It was easier if he didn't look at her. "I have... something I'd like to say. To *ask.*"

He felt Greta's gaze on him, doe-like eyes fixed on his face. Was her expression curios or confused? Excited or nervous? Did she have any inclination of what he was about to ask? Yet she said nothing, which only made anxiety coil further into his stomach.

A couple wandered past, arm in arm. The woman's skirt billowed about her ankles as she walked, the man's hair rustling in the gentle wind. They barely spared a look for Billy or Greta, too wrapped up in each other. He wondered if he looked like that with Greta.

Finally, he couldn't put it off any more. The silence stretched on, becoming awkward as they walked. Clearing his throat, Billy said, "You know I broke up with Holly? I told you it was a long time coming, and that much is true. That... that wasn't all, though."

A gentle hand on his shoulder, a smile meant only for him. Seeing Greta smile like that never failed to make his heart skip. "I don't claim its my business to know - but whatever it is, I promise I won't judge you."

Judgement wasn't his worry. *Rejection* was; but he was a grown man, capable of handling it. So, with a deep breath and no time to regret his decision he blurted, "we broke up because I'm in love with you. I didn't realise it at the time, but it's true. *I love you, Greta.*"

Halting mid step, she turned to him with wide, sparkling eyes. "Do you mean it?"

"Of course. I wouldn't make this up."

For a moment, he truly worried she might leave. Had he gone too far? Scared her off? Misjudged her feelings for him? There were a million reasons he could have messed up, and each one whirled around in his mind.

Until Greta's soft lips touched his own. It was barely a kiss, her soft skin ghosting across his, lips crooking into a smile as she pressed them to his. "I've loved you for eight years, you know."

Billy's mind went blank. *Eight years.* That meant... she had loved him since the day they met. Even while she was still with Mark, her husband.

"I realised I'd likely never see you again," she continued quietly, placing another kiss against his cheek. Her breath was warm and smelled like sweetened coffee. "It didn't stop me from wishing, though."

"But Mark-"

"Gave me Hannah, for which I'll always be grateful; but I always knew, from the beginning, that you and I were meant for each other."

The urge to laugh rose in his throat, pulse racing in his ears. He grinned wide, arms encasing Greta - but then the moment shattered. His dark eyes fixed on someone across the road; someone wearing a yellow summer dress and storming right toward them.

Holly. Here to make good on her threats.

"Greta," he murmured, turning to block her view of Holly, "are you hungry? Why don't we get something to eat?"

"I ate this afternoon," she admitted, brows raised, "anyway, why the sudden-"

Too late. Already Holly was closing the distance, her heels clicking on the stone path. She tossed golden curls over her shoulder, and her smile turned wicked. "Oh look, my two least favourite people. *Just* who I've been looking for."

Billy paled. So did Greta, but she couldn't have known who Holly was. Maybe she knew just from the tone of voice. Slowly they both turned, Billy's arm around her waist, as Holly trotted to a stop in front of them.

"How did you know we were here?"

"I asked around," Holly answered with a shrug, "this town is so tiny and drab, there weren't many places to choose from." Hands on her hip, she let her gaze rove across Greta. "Really. *This* is who you left me for. Plain, isn't she? At least her hair is pretty-"

"Holly, now isn't the time."

"Which is precisely why I'm here. There was a rumour going around that you planned on asking her out - that's the problem with sharing a friend circle with your ex."

They were never *his* friends, and that was the problem, but Billy kept his mouth shut.

Beside him, Greta tensed. "Billy, what's going on?"

"Don't cause a scene, Holly," Billy hissed, eyes darting about the park. There weren't many people here - a few couples, a father with his kid, a handful of solitary people out for a walk. It was *enough,* though, and he knew gossip travelled fast in this town. "It's been weeks, I thought-"

"You thought wrong." Holly's smile was sickly sweet, her lips painted a shade of pale pink Billy had always loved. Now, it looked as fake as her smile.

Greta tugged on his sleeve, wide eyes darting between them both. "Holly, isn't it? I'm sorry, I never meant to cause problems-"

"This isn't about *you,"* Holly snapped, "you're just a tiny fraction of this whole mess. He was supposed to be *mine,* but instead he's hanging onto the arm of some Amish woman-"

"Holly. *Enough.*" His voice rang out throughout the park - a few heads turned, unblinking eyes staring at them like they were acting out a play. Forcing his voice lower, he muttered, "I'm not the only one who messed up here. You need to take some accountability too. I wouldn't have left if I was happy with you, would I?"

Her lips parted, but no sound came out. Instead she huffed, rolling her eyes like he was a child that had said something silly. Like she was *humouring him.* Then, "you and I, we had something good. But *her?* If you can't love me, you'll never love her."

Silence. It was as if even the birds had stopped, and all Billy heard was the ringing of his own pulse in his ears. It was *deafening.* He wanted to shout, to tell Holly to leave and never so much as *look* at either of them again - but he couldn't bring himself to speak.

The silence shattered when Greta stumbled back, letting out a cry as her foot hit an uneven stone in the path. She wobbled, righted herself, and then turned heel and *ran.* By the time Billy's mind had shifted back into gear, she was already half way across the park.

"You've gone too far this time, Holly." Voice eerily calm, it didn't sound like his at all. He stared her down, and for the first time she actually *flinched* under his gaze. "You can't *keep me,* not any more than I can keep Greta. I made my choice. Deal with it."

Her eyes watered, but she blinked it away before tears could fall. Of course. Holly didn't *do* vulnerable. Instead she scowled, but it was a weak attempt. "We could have been happy. Why ruin it all?"

"We weren't happy," he replied sharply, "Greta just helped me see that."

"You and her won't last. You'll get bored, or she'll want rid of you just like her last husband-"

"I'm not Mark, and she isn't *you.* We won't repeat past mistakes."

The last of her anger drained, along with the colour from her face. Had it finally sank in? That they were *over* for good? She stepped back, heels clicking, and let her arms drop to her side. Defeated. "Go after her then, if you love her so much. I'm done with all of this, I never want to see her - or you - again."

The feeling's mutual, he wanted to say - but there was no time. With one last glance toward Holly, he sped off down across the park - toward where Greta had gone. People stared as he sprinted, no doubt some of them had overheard their argument. So what? Greta was the only thing that mattered.

Billy found her under the canopy of a cluster of redwoods, head in her hands as she curled in on herself. Her cheeks were dry as she looked up at him, but with the way her eyes watered they wouldn't remain so for long. "Talk things out with her?" she asked dully.

"Sort of." Settling down beside her, he ignored how uncomfortable the hard earth was. "She won't bother us any more."

"How do you know?"

"Because I know Holly. Too well, actually."

A smile curled at the edges of her lips; even with her messy hair and watery eyes, Greta was beautiful. "I didn't mean to put you through all of this, you know. If I'd known what she would do, I wouldn't have-"

"I brought it on myself," Billy replied gently. He tugged her close, letting her drop her head onto his broad shoulder. It was the most comfortable he had been in a long time. "It isn't your fault. Not even a bit."

"It still feels like it is," she huffed. Yet she snuggled into him, ignoring the curious looks from an old man a few meters away. It was probably improper, or whatever people called it - but neither of them cared.

"I should be the one apologising to you," Billy stated, "I mean, I didn't think she's really cause a scene, but she's been throwing threats at me for weeks."

"It doesn't matter any more. Not when we have each other."

As soon as she said it, Billy knew it was true. He brushed his lips against her forehead, revelling in the softness of her. They had each other, and that was what mattered. He grinned as Greta tilted her head up, allowing him to kiss her properly. She tasted of that sugary coffee, smelled of grass and flowers, and he could have become lost in her.

Then the old man coughed, jolting them from their reverie. Face flushed, Greta ducked into the crook of his neck. "Maybe now isn't the time," she murmured.

"Maybe," he replied softly, "but I don't care."

Then he kissed her again, hands tangling in her golden hair, her laughter tickling his lips, and everything else just disappeared.

AMISH DEPARTURE

DEIDRA SCOTT

Chapter One

Lizzy Swartz closed her eyes and took in a deep breath of the spring air. The scent of cut grass and freshly plowed dirt put a smile on her face. She lifted her face upward, allowing the sun to warm her skin.

There was nothing like a spring day spent working out in the garden. Just the time in God's outdoors put a song in Lizzy's heart.

Suddenly, something hard hit her in the arm. Lizzy opened her eyes to see her fifteen-year-old brother, Abe, preparing to launch another clod of dirt in her direction.

"*Ach*, Abe!" Lizzy exclaimed, "Will ya never start to grow up?"

Abe stood up straighter and gave his dirt ball a toss across the garden, "Probably not," he replied, a boyish grin spreading across his handsome face.

Lizzy couldn't help but smile back, "Well, don't just stand there – pick up a garden hoe and get to work!"

"Yes, ma'am!" Abe returned in a silly tone and anxiously grabbed one of the tools, "I wouldn't want you to decide to whack me *gut* with one."

"Where's Grandpa?" Lizzy asked as she set to work chopping out some of the weeds that were starting to grow between the rows.

"He ran out to the mailbox," Abe replied.

They worked in silence for a few minutes until Abe finally asked, "Lizzy, what do you think would have happened to us if Grandpa hadn't taken us in?"

Abe's question made Lizzy stop for a moment. My, but hadn't she asked herself that question at least a dozen times? It had been almost twelve years since their parents had been killed in a tragic buggy wreck. The Amish community had been hit by hard times already with a rough drought that killed most of the area crops and left everyone feeling the strain financially. No one had enough money to take on two extra Amish children. At one point, there had been talk of sending Lizzy and Abe to foster care...but then Grandpa had stepped in.

A widower who was already shouldering the heavy job of being bishop to the Amish community, Grandpa had taken them in as if they were his own children. Although they called him Grandpa, he was completely unrelated to Lizzy and Abe.

"I don't know, Abe," Lizzy finally said with a deep sigh, "But I certainly thank God every day for sending him our way."

Abe slowly nodded his head, "*Jah*, me too."

They both worked in silence.

Grandpa had not provided them with a fancy life full of impressive possessions, but he had done his part to give them a stable home that was rich in love. Over the years, he had worked hard to instill steady morals, a love for their Creator, and a respect for hard work in the hearts of both Lizzy and her brother.

"Have you got any plans for tonight?" Abe finally asked.

Lizzy felt her face go red with embarrassment. "*Ach*, Abe," she exclaimed, "Aren't you a nosey one! Maybe I do and maybe I don't!"

"I already know you're going out with Matt Christner!" Abe exclaimed, tossing another clod of dirt at his sister, "I saw him in town and he told me."

"Well, isn't he the big mouth!" Lizzy returned with a laugh.

While Lizzy and Matt had been friends for most of their lives, they had only recently started dating. Although their relationship was new, Lizzy had already recognized that Matt was the man she wanted to eventually marry.

Lizzy's thoughts were cut short when she heard Grandpa whistling as he walked up behind her.

"Mail's here!" He announced cheerfully as he handed Lizzy a letter from her cousin in Pennsylvania.

"Didn't I get anything?" Abe asked.

"You can open mine," Grandpa told him with a laugh, tossing a handful of envelopes in his direction, "Let me know if I got anything other than bills. I'm going out to the calf barn to check on some of the babies."

Abe flipped the mail around in his hand, sorting through it for anything exciting. Stopping at one envelope, he gave a shrug and tore it open.

"Oh, Abe," Lizzy let out a laugh as she started to read the letter from her cousin, "Sally says..."

"Wait, Lizzy!" Abe exclaimed, cutting her short. Before she could protest, he called out, "Grandpa, come back here! It's important!"

Grandpa turned and hurried back to Abe's side, anxious to see what was wrong.

"*Ach*, what's happened now?" He asked, reaching for the letter.

"It nothing bad, Grandpa!" Abe exclaimed, "Its good news! Your uncle who died left you a lot of money! A lot! Yee-haw!"

"Well, I'll be," Grandpa whispered as he scanned over the document, "It surely does look like I've inherited quite a sum of money...from an uncle I don't even remember."

As Grandpa read the letter once more, Abe gave his hat a toss in the air and grabbed his sister by the shoulders, "Lizzy...we're rich!"

Chapter Two

Until Grandpa had a chance to go see the lawyer in town, they all three agreed not to tell a soul about the letter or the possibility of the inheritance. While Abe was convinced that they truly were now wealthy, neither Lizzy nor Grandpa shared his confidence.

That night, Lizzy's boyfriend Matt arrived at their house on his buggy. Although it was hard to think of anything other than the inheritance, getting to go somewhere with Matt seemed like it might distract her from the thought of money.

As she rode along beside Matt on his buggy, Lizzy found that the idea of getting her mind on something else was entirely too far-fetched to be possible.

Suddenly, Lizzy realized that Matt had hardly spoken a word to her since he picked her up at her house.

"*Ach*, Matt," she muttered, suddenly feeling ashamed of herself, "Here we've been riding together for miles and I've hardly spoken a word this whole trip. I'm sorry. I'd better watch it or you'll be picking you out a new sweetheart!"

Turning to look at Matt, she realized that he wasn't laughing or even smiling at her comments. Instead, it seemed like a dark cloud was over his handsome face.

"You shouldn't be apologizing, Lizzy," Matt replied with a deep sigh as he turned the reigns over in his hands, "I should be the one doing that. I'm not much company tonight. Probably not the best day to be takin' ya out to eat, but I sure hated to cancel. Wouldn't want you to pick out a new beau either."

Studying her boyfriend's sad face made Lizzy feel like crying herself. She knew that her Matt had been going through a rough year. His mom had been diagnosed with cancer and, although the treatments seemed to be working, Lizzy realized the family was still dealing with a lot of stress and uncertainty.

Reaching out to pat him on the shoulder, Lizzy found herself searching for the right words to say but coming up short.

"Matt," she finally said with a sigh, "The Lord hasn't forgotten about your family – he has a plan."

Matt slowly nodded his head, but Lizzy wondered if his faith was getting shaky.

The next morning, Grandpa got up early to hitch up the buggy and drive into town to see a lawyer. Although Grandpa warned Lizzy and Abe that the letter was probably nothing more than just a fake, it was impossible not to notice the hopeful glimmer in his eyes.

Waiting for Grandpa to get home was about enough to drive Lizzy mad. The hours seemed to pass so slowly and, every time Lizzy glanced toward the driveway, her heart sank as she realized Grandpa was no where in sight.

Trying to make the time pass faster, Lizzy busied herself with chores around the house. By afternoon, Lizzy had already scrubbed all of the hardwood floors, hosed off the porch, and washed the windows.

"Still no sign of Grandpa?" Abe asked as he stepped into the kitchen, looking for an afternoon snack.

Lizzy shook her head as she lowered one of the windows, "I hope he's okay."

The barking of their dog sent both Lizzy and Abe to the front door.

"He's home!" Abe squealed, jumping like a little kid as he pushed past Lizzy and started out toward the barn where Grandpa was unhitching the horses.

Not wanting to be left out, Lizzy followed close behind her brother.

By the time they reached the barn, both Lizzy and Abe were out of breath.

"Grandpa," Abe gasped, grabbing his side with his hand, "Grandpa, what happened? What did he say?"

"Help me unhitch the horses, Abe," Grandpa replied solemnly as his leathery hands set to work taking the bits out of the animals' mouths.

Abe stepped up and started working alongside his grandfather, his mouth still going much faster than his fingers, "But Grandpa, what happened in town?"

"*Ach*, Abe, we'll talk once we're all inside."

"But we're all out here, Grandpa!"

Despite Abe's pleading, Grandpa remained firm. Watching him lead the horses to an empty stall where he poured them some fresh oats, Lizzy felt her heart sink. There was no way the letter could have been true.

Once they were finished, Grandpa sat down at the kitchen table while Lizzy hurried to set a plate of fresh cookies and a glass of milk in front of him.

"Sit down, Lizzy. Sit down, Abe." Grandpa instructed.

Abe practically jumped into his seat and Lizzy felt like she couldn't grab the chair fast enough.

"Children," Grandpa finally said with a laugh, "I don't know how to tell you this...but the letter was real and the money is now in the bank. We truly are rich!"

Chapter Three

While Grandpa wouldn't say just how much money he had inherited, Lizzy realized that it must be a lot.

Sitting around the table that night, Grandpa explained that the money was something they needed to use for good purposes.

"I know how easy it is to simply waste money," Grandpa told them as he finished off Lizzy's delicious meal of homemade sweet rolls, applesauce, fried potatoes, and pork chops, "And I don't want us to waste what we have now. Before we start spending a lot of it, I want you two to come up with some ways that we could use the money to do something *gut*...not just for ourselves, but for the entire community."

Abe lowered his head, obviously a bit disappointed at the thought of having to share with the rest of the Amish.

"Can we buy a few things for ourselves?" Abe asked with 'humph'.

"Of course," Grandpa opened up his wallet and began sorting through his bills, "I know that there are things around the house that we need. Lizzy," he motioned for her to hold out her hand, "This is for you and Abe to spend on the things that we need."

Unfolding the bills that Grandpa had placed in her hand, Lizzy gasped as she whispered, "*Ach*, Grandpa, this is one-thousand dollars!"

Grandpa nodded slowly, "I think it's time that we made some improvements around here. Let me know if you need more than that."

Staring at the money, Lizzy wondered how on earth she could ever begin to think of spending one-thousand dollars on anything.

The next morning, Lizzy discovered that spending money was much easier than she had expected. When she had her driver take her to the grocery store, she planned to only spend within her usual budget. For the last five years, Grandpa had given Lizzy the sole responsibility of shopping for their weekly groceries with a very small amount of money. Lizzy had learned how to be resourceful by making purchases in bulk, off-brand items, and using coupons.

As she entered the store that Thursday morning, it seemed harder than ever to stick to her budget. Just knowing that she had one-thousand dollars to use as she saw fit made shopping seem like an entirely different experience.

When she left the grocery, Lizzy had a cart load full of groceries she would never normally purchase. After seeing how high the bils was, Lizzy promised herself she would start using their money more wisely.

Despite Lizzy's resolution to be more careful with the money, it seemed less possible with each day that passed.

Grandpa and Abe were astonished with her expensive meals that included thick steaks, but enjoyed them so much that she wasn't scolded; in fact, Grandpa reminded her to keep buying what they needed because the money was unlimited.

Although Lizzy had always enjoyed baking, the convenience of running to the store to pick up ready-to-eat loaves of bread, pies, and cookies was almost more than she could stand.

When wash day came, Lizzy even hired a driver to take her to the local laundry mat where she was able to get them cleaned and dried in a fraction of the time it took her to do the job by hand at home.

As soon as Lizzy realized that some of their clothing needed to be patched, she chose to toss the damaged items in the trash rather than keep them. When she went to pick out new fabric, the thought of sewing sounded so time consuming, that she simply hired one of the local Amish seamstresses to do the work for her.

While her work load dwindled, Lizzy took the opportunity to enjoy time reading books and going on walks in the fields.

Lizzy wasn't the only one who enjoyed the chance to indulge in some expensive luxuries. Grandpa decided that, rather than clean out the barn by hand, he would hire someone with a bobcat to do it for him.

"We need to make some serious barn repairs, too." Grandpa told Abe and Lizzy, "I'm thinking we could just hire a team of the Amish carpenters to come fix it up for us." Pausing for a moment to think, he added, "Honestly, might be even more sensible to just build a new barn all together."

"Grandpa," Luke started slowly, "I'll be sixteen next month and the age to go to the young peoples' gatherings. Do ya suppose you could just buy me a new buggy to drive? The old one's so worn out and it sure sends me in the air when I hit a bump – I'd hate to find me a pretty girl and send her sailing off the buggy seat!"

They all laughed and Grandpa nodded, "*Jah*, I don't see how a new buggy could hurt!"

Within a few days, the entire family wondered how they had ever lived on such a tight budget in the past.

Chapter Four

Saturday night, Lizzy and Matt went out on a date to the local *Englisher* restaurant in town. Whenever they went out to eat, it was a treat, but today seemed somewhat less of a thrill. With all the money that Lizzy had been spending on fancy food to cook at home, the meal seemed rather boring.

Once they had finished eating, the waitress came by and asked, "Do you want to order some desert?"

Looking at Lizzy with a smile, Matt announced, "I guess we'll take a piece of chocolate cake with ice-cream. We're splitting it, so we'll need an extra plate."

"*Ach*, Matt, sharing is such a bother." Lizzy couldn't hide her disgust at the thought of being frugal, "Let's get one for each of us!"

"Lizzy," Matt reached out and put his hand over hers, his tone little more than a whisper, "I don't have the money..."

"Don't worry about paying for it, Matt," Lizzy announced, digging through her black purse for some money, "I'll be covering the bill tonight."

Looking up at the waitress, Matt said, "Just give us one. If we need more, I'll buy a second."

The waitress looked uncomfortably from Matt to Lizzy and then back to Matt. Taking a deep breath, she nodded her head, "I'll put in the order for one. Just flag me down if you decide to get two."

As soon as she had left them alone, Lizzy found herself rolling her eyes, "Come on, Matt! What's the matter? I said I have the money. Why can't you let me pay for it myself?"

Matt shook his head slowly, "Lizzy, you don't understand. I don't want to have a girlfriend that pays for her own food. I like saving back my money and bringing you out to eat."

Unwilling to cause a scene or risk totally running their time together, Lizzy gave a curt nod and ended the conversation.

When the waitress delivered their cake, they ate in silence. Lizzy simply could not understand why her boyfriend was so stubborn!

"I'm sorry we fought in the restaurant," Matt whispered when they had finished eat and were seated side-by-side on his buggy, "I don't want us to ever argue about anything. Will ya forgive me...and still let me bring you to the young peoples' meeting Sunday night?"

Lizzy couldn't help but smile. Staying mad at her boyfriend wasn't worth the effort. Sliding over closer to him, she took a deep breath, "I'm sorry, too. *Ach*, Matt, I never would have brought up paying for it if I knew it was going to make you upset." Leaning her head against his shoulder, she took a deep breath of the night air and wished that there was some way that he, too, could enjoy the money her family had been given.

The next morning, Lizzy, Grandpa, and Abe went to church at Joe Eicher's house. Like all Amish people, the community met every other week at one of the homes of an Amish family. Preparing for the church service was a huge event that generally involved hours of cleaning and set-up.

On the way to the Eicher's house, Lizzy noticed Grandpa eyeing various things along the road. When they went past the Amish schoolhouse, he slowed the buggy down to a crawl as he pointed out the sagging roof and needed repairs.

During they church service, Lizzy watched Grandpa stare absent-mindedly at his hands. As bishop of their Amish community, Grandpa was not in charge of preaching but rather helped the entire group stay true to their beliefs.

Once they had sung the last song and church was ready to end, Grandpa stood up and raise a hand in the air.

"Before we go out to eat this delicious meal, I have an announcement to make," Grandpa said.

At his words, women stopped gathering their children and everyone returned to their seats to listen quietly to what their leader had to say.

"As everyone here knows, I've never been a rich man," Grandpa announced, "So you can imagine my surprise this past week when I discovered that I have inherited a large sum of money."

Lizzy listened as the Amish began to whisper and buzz with excitement.

"Driving past the school house today, I noticed that it needs some serious repairs." Reaching into his billfold, Grandpa pulled out a check,

"That's why I want to call Teacher Simon forward to receive a check for twenty-thousand dollars to make the necessary repairs."

Everyone gasped and then began to clap their hands.

"*Wunderbargut*!" Someone yelled out in excitement, "The children won't have to worry about it raining in on their heads any longer!" Everyone laughed.

Giving the congregation a chance to settle down, Grandpa finally announced, "I have something else to bring up, too. I know that this is different, but I want everyone here to take some time to consider this suggestion. My whole life, I've watched the women in our community burdened with the heavy load of hosting church service at their homes. I propose that we step out and build a new church building."

Suddenly, the room went silent.

Build a church? Even to Lizzy, the idea sounded strange and terribly English! Although she saw nothing wrong with the big, impressive churches in the towns, it wasn't their way at all. The Amish were simple folks and holding church within the homes was a tradition that went back hundreds of years.

As the minutes ticked by, there was still no reply to his suggestion. Finally, Joe Eicher stepped up, uncomfortably putting his hands in his pockets and refusing to look at Grandpa, "We'll have a chance to talk about all these things later. For now, my wife invites you outside to have a picnic in our front yard."

Chapter Five

Grandpa didn't stay for the picnic; instead he suggested that they stop at the restaurant in town to buy some food. Lizzy missed the feeling of togetherness she got when she gathered with her friends and family, but certainly wasn't sad to avoid the awkward stares of the others in her community.

That night, Matt pulled his buggy into their driveway at five o'clock. Lizzy had purchased some pre-made hamburger patties in town and had just finished frying them up for her Grandpa and Abe. She would eat at the young peoples' gathering.

"You're making me hungry already," Matt playfully moaned as he leaned over her shoulder. Picking up the box the patties came in, he announced, "*Ach*, we never buy these – too expensive for us poor folks." Although his words were said as a joke, Lizzy noticed something akin to scorn in his voice.

"Who could be here?" Lizzy wondered as she noticed three buggies full of Amish men pull into their drive.

Matt gave a shrug, "Looks like some of the preachers and leaders of the community."

Although she knew it was wrong to spy, Lizzy watched the men hitch their horses to the post by the porch and then step through the front door.

"Hello, Abe," she heard the men greet her brother as they walked through the front door, "Where is your grandpa?"

Lizzy picked up the plate of hamburgers and took them to the table where Grandpa was sitting just as Abe led the group of men into the room.

"Hello there, Mose," the men greeted Grandpa, "Sorry to interrupt your meal."

"No worries," Grandpa returned, "Take chairs. What's on your minds?"

As the men sat down, Lizzy and Matt stepped back into the corner, anxious to see what would happen and hoping not to be sent out of the room.

"*Ach*, Mose," one of the men finally said, "Have you plumb lost your mind?"

"Easy now, Enos," another spoke up, "Mose, we were so thankful for your contribution to the schoolhouse, but I'm afraid that I'm with Enos in asking, what were you thinking when you brought up building a church? You know that isn't the Amish way!"

Grandpa raised an eyebrow, "Come on, men! You know there's no good reason for us not to have a church building."

"Having church within the homes sets us apart from the *Englicher* world," Sam Yoder announced, "If you pull out one of the threads of our beliefs, soon we'll completely unravel! What will keep us from soon having telephones and electricity?"

"And what would be so wrong with that?" Grandpa exclaimed suddenly. In the fifteen years that Lizzy had lived with Grandpa, she had never seen him so upset about anything. She felt almost frightened as she looked into his angry face and watched as it grew redder by the minute.

The other men's eyes grew large as they stared at him.

"Ach," Grandpa finally stormed, "You don't have to like my suggestions at all, but I'll say this...building a church would help our community, and I *am* going to do it! As the bishop of our community, I have the power and with the money, I have the ability."

If the men had looked surprised before, they were totally speechless now. Finally, Enos Bontrager solemnly announced, "I'm sorry you feel this way, Mose. It seems the money has gone to your brain. You maybe the bishop of our community, but that does not mean that you are above reproach. Take some time to consider this idea of yours. If you don't submit to the Amish ways, I'm afraid the community will be forced to go over your head and inflict the *bann*."

The *bann*. Those dreadful words went through Lizzy's mind over and over again. Although she was sitting beside Matt on his buggy, she couldn't pull her thoughts away from that horrible scene at the kitchen table.

Ach, if the Amish chose to *bann* Grandpa, he would be completely forced from their community. He would not longer be able to eat with them – he would be entirely shunned until he repented publicly.

"What's going on with your grandpa, Lizzy?" Matt asked after taking a deep breath, obviously nervous to bring up the uncomfortable subject, "He used to be one of the easiest-going men I ever knew...now he's just acting ornery about everything!"

Lizzy instantly felt her skin bristle. Who was Matt to call her Grandpa names?

"What's that supposed to mean?" She spoke up.

"Come on, Lizzy!" Matt exclaimed, "He's changed...and you have too! Just within a week, it's like you're both different people. I don't like who you're turning into. If things don't change, he's going to end up leaving the Amish entirely."

Lizzy was so furious, it felt like she was on fire.

"Grandpa is one of the best men I know!" She snapped, "If he wants to build a church building, then I'm completely behind him. If you have a problem with it, then maybe we should stop seeing each other. And, if the Amish are going to be so stubborn that they won't accept his gift, then maybe I don't want to be Amish anymore!"

"Lizzy..."

"Just drive," She snapped, folding her arms across her chest and scooting as far away from her boyfriend as she could.

That night, Lizzy sat in her bedroom, thinking about life as she prepared for bed. Lizzy brushed her hair out slowly and stopped to study herself in the mirror. While mirrors weren't usually found in Amish houses, Lizzy had made a secret purchase over the weekend.

Gazing at herself, she tried to gauge how pretty she was compared to the other Amish girls. But wouldn't she be prettier if she had some of that fine paint the *Englishers* wore on their faces!

Instantly, she pushed the thought away, wishing that she hadn't let it run through her mind.

With all that was going on with her grandfather, she truly wondered if they would be left in the Amish church. What Matt had repeated was what all the Amish were thinking. Grandpa was determined to go forward with his plans to build a church...and the Amish community wasn't going to stand for it. There was a good chance that they might get shunned. If that happened, she wondered what Grandpa would do. Would he turn his back on the Amish way entirely? And, if he did, would she go with him?

"Lizzy, Lizzy," she scolded herself, "What are you a thinkin'? Consider Matt!"

But, the more she considered Matt, the more clouded her thinking became. She had been so certain that he was the man she wanted to marry and spend the rest of her life beside, but the money had changed everything.

Lizzy was beginning to like the feeling that money gave her. It made her happy to know that she and her family were a step above the rest of those in their community. She was tired of the work that she had to do as an Amish woman.

If they left the Amish, she would be free to own a washing machine and a drier, a refrigerator, and even a television! Putting aside her brush, Lizzy ran her hand through her hair and took a deep breath.

She was almost scared of what tomorrow might bring.

Chapter Six

All Monday morning, Lizzy found herself looking out the window, afraid that she would see more of the church leaders coming up the drive. In some ways she was frightened, while in others she was almost hopeful.

Grandpa sat at the table, working on a design for the new church. Since the Amish community was set against having it built, he had already contacted a team of English carpenters who could do the work.

That afternoon, someone finally did come up the drive. When Lizzy saw that it was Matt, she couldn't decide if she was more relieved or disgusted.

"Lizzy," Matt took off his straw hat and twisted it between his hands when she invited him inside, "Could we go on a walk and talk?"

Preparing for a lecture, Lizzy braced herself and started across the yard beside him.

Suddenly, Lizzy was surprised when she looked up at Matt and noticed tear drops running down his cheeks. Instantly, her defenses were down and her heart filled with worry for this man she loved so much.

"What's wrong Matt?" Lizzy asked as she reached out to pat her boyfriend on the arm,

"Lizzy," Matt took a deep breath and let it out, "I don't know what to say. My *maam*'s finally going to come home, but now the hospital wants us to start paying our bills. She's got to keep taking treatments and they're expensive, too. Dad doesn't even know how he's going to do it at all. He's talking about selling the farm."

"Selling the farm!" Lizzy exclaimed, "What would you all do then?"

"*Daed*'s talking about moving back to Pennsylvania. There's nothing for us here if we have to sell everything. We can move in with my grandparents until mom's treatments are finished."

"Surely there will be some other way..."

"Lizzy, my dad already took out a gigantic mortgage on the farm. He's not going to be able to pay it back." Shrugging, Matt announced, "I don't know when we're likely to move, but I'd like the little bit of time we have left together to be good. I'm sorry about last night."

"No, I'm sorry," Lizzy whispered. Reaching out, she wrapped her arms around her boyfriend and pulled him close to her.

That night, Lizzy picked up some food at the restaurant because she didn't feel like cooking. Her heart felt so heavy whenever she thought about Matt and his family. She told Grandpa and Abe. Suddenly, they were no longer concerned about building fancy churches or fighting with the Amish. They just sat together silently, each lost in sorrow over the situation of Matt's family.

"I wish that there was something we could do," Abe muttered softly, "I've always though a lot of Matt's family."

"*Ach*," Grandpa exclaimed as he slammed his hand against the tabletop, "What on earth are we doing? I always looked down on people who had money and were selfish with it...and yet I find that I'm exactly the same way."

"Grandpa!" Abe looked at him in surprise, "How can you say that you're selfish? All you want to do with your money is good! You want to make a better life for us...and you want to help out the church and the community with buildings. How can that be wrong?"

Grandpa shook his head slowly, "In the midst of all our figuring, did we ever stop to even think to ask the Lord what He would want us to do with this money? No. Instead, we chose to plow ahead and do what we thought was best."

Everyone was silent as they looked down at their plates in deep thought.

"Tonight, this ends!" Grandpa announced, reaching out to take Abe's hand in one of his own and Lizzy's in the other, "Tonight we're turning to the Lord to find out what he wants."

The next morning, Grandpa took the money that Lizzy had left over and went to town.

"Well," Abe muttered softly as he worked alongside his sister in the garden, "I sure did enjoy being rich."

"As did I," Lizzy said with a sigh, "But I think I'll be glad to be plain Lizzy once again."

When Grandpa got home, he came out to the garden to work alongside them.

No one said a word until Abe finally ventured to ask, "Do we have anything left at all?"

Grandpa shook his head, "I paid off all of Matt's family's debts and then gave the rest as a donation to the hospital. I've already been to talk to some of the church leaders and apologized for the entire church building idea."

"How are we ever going to make it now?" Abe grumbled, kicking at a clod of dirt with the toe of his work boots.

Grandpa smiled, "I suppose the way we always have...a lot of pinching pennies and patching up clothes. In the end, we did what that Lord wanted and we did what was best for other people who needed the money much worse than us."

"I never did get my buggy," Abe said with a sigh.

"Ahh...that is true." Grandpa gave the teenager a pat on the shoulder, "How about you and I work on that old buggy together. I think if we put some time into it, we can have it good as new."

"And, when you go courting, maybe you can just tell her to hang on tight before you hit a bump in the road!" Lizzy suggested.

They all laughed, finally able to enjoy one another's company without the distraction of money.

Working together silently, they listened to the sound of the birds chirping overhead and enjoyed the cool breeze drifting through the trees.

Prologue

Lizzy smiled to herself as she sat on the homemade wooden swing on the front porch. Although it had been hard to give up the money, she had to admit that a simple life truly was the right one for her.

Looking up from a page in the book she was reading, Lizzy realized that Matt had pulled his buggy into their yard and was coming toward her.

"Hello, Matt," she announced, wishing that she and her beau had never gone through such a rough spot.

Without saying a word, Matt took a seat on the swing beside her.

"It was your grandpa, wasn't it?" Matt asked slowly as he reached out and took Lizzy's hand in his own, "He was the one who helped to cover my *maam*'s doctor bills, right?"

"Matt..." Lizzy looked down at her feet, trying to decide how much she should even start to share, "Ach, Matt, he doesn't want a bunch of people to know. He wanted to keep it a secret. The way Grandpa looks at it, the money wasn't ours to start with...it was just something that God had loaned us so that we could use it to help others. He got off track because of it...we all did, I'm afraid. I'm sorry that I was so harsh to ya, Matt. It was wrong of me. I let the love of money cloud my thinking. Grandpa reminded us that we should pray about what to do with it, and from that point on, it all just became clear."

Matt shook his head, "That's the kind of man I wish that I could be. Lizzy," he took a deep breath, "I'm no where near as great a man as your grandpa, but I'm going to try my best to be a *gut* Amish man who loves his family, helps his neighbors, and serves the Lord. Would you be willing to go through this journey with me...as my wife?"

Lizzy felt her breath catch in her throat and she wondered if she could even start to speak. After all that had happened between them, she was afraid that Matt would be ready to end their relationship completely. She opened her mouth and words wouldn't come out. Instead, all that would come were tears of joy.

"Oh no," Matt teased jokingly, "Looks like you're not very happy with my question!"

Lizzy threw her arms around his neck and let her warm embrace give her answer. Pulling away from the man that she loved, Lizzy exclaimed, "Ah, Matt, being married to you is going to be better than all the money in the world!"

AMISH CHRISTMAS MIRACLE

MONICA MARKS

Amish Christmas Miracle

"I am rather looking forward to springtime again," Jacob grumbled as they sloshed through the sleet. "I loathe to wear such heavy boots with woolen socks. I am counting the days until my feet are bare night and day!"

Janey sighed and shook her long, dark mane of curls.

"How can you say that, Jacob? It is the end of fall, we have just been through the wedding season and Christmas is at our doorstep. This time of year is the most magical!"

Jacob grimaced as his foot landed in another puddle, the two making their way through the aftermath of a storm toward the schoolhouse.

"I do not know how women maintain such a fascination with weddings and Christmas but I find them both tiresome and consuming from a time and energy viewpoint. I want for the warmth of the summer sun."

"I must say you sound just like Ebenezer Scrooge in *A Christmas Carol*. How can you be so miserable?"

Jacob laughed and the friends exchanged a pretend scowl but both knew that Jacob was merely exaggerating his despise of the cold seasons.

It was true, however, that Janey was much more avid about the winter months than him.

They had grown up together, Jane Byler and Jacob Epp. Their ages had ensured them close in school and both their families ran dairy farms, often pooling their resources together for better profit.

Jacob's sister Eva was the same age as Janey's brother, David, ensuring an even closer bond between the families if ever there needed be one.

The Bylers and the Epps were as close as two families in the district could be.

It was assumed then, that Jacob and Janey would announce their engagement soon after their baptisms but much to everyone's surprise, Janey found the notion preposterous.

Imagine, marrying Jacob Epp, Janey often thought, staring at the fair-haired boy with adoration. *It would be no different than marrying David when he came of age! How could anyone believe that he and I would ever consider such a path? We are more like brother and sister than two fated to be wed.*

No, there was no announcement of marriage destined to befall Jacob and Janey but that did not stop Janey from aspiring toward finding her perfect match.

The question was, who was he and when would he surface?

It seemed highly unlikely that she had already met her future husband.

Janey and her peers had already taken part in the tradition of *Rumspringa* and it seemed as soon as the baptism ceremonies had been conducted, her single friends had become engaged women.

"You are so lucky!" Janey gushed to them. "Soon you will be wed with little ones on the way. I wonder if I will ever find the same happiness."

Inevitably, the girls would laugh and pat her arm.

"Oh, Janey, everyone knows you are going to marry Jacob Epp. Why do you fight against *Gotte's* plan?"

Janey would smile softly and shake her dark curls, marveling at how people she had known since infancy could know so little about her.

They do not know what they are taking about. Jacob is my truest friend but he is just that and only that.

Janey often wondered if Jacob was ribbed in the same way by the boys. She imagined so.

This year, I will get them to eat their words once and for all. This year I will have found a suitor by Christmas. A suitor not Jacob.

The bell began to toll as the duo made their way through the muddy field toward the schoolhouse and immediately, the doors spilled open.

Two dozen children ran from the single school room, chattering excitedly as they carried their books, splashing through the mud where Jane and Jacob had tried so carefully to avoid it.

Jacob caught sight of his eleven-year-old sister and waved her over to where they stood.

As always, ten-year-old David was in her shadow and they trudged toward their siblings.

"It is becoming embarrassing," Eva sighed as she approached. "I am almost finished school and yet you are still here to walk me from school every afternoon!"

Janey stifled a smile, ruffling her brother's soft curls as he approached at his own turtle's pace.

"You have two more years of schooling, Eva," Jacob replied, a note of exasperation in his voice. "And I assure you, I could imagine better things to do with my afternoon than coming to walk you home."

"But Jacob, why does *Dat* insist on you coming every single day?" Eva asked in her childlike way, her lower lip extended in a slight pout.

Dear Gotte, if she was only a bit older or Jacob a decade younger, they would be impossible to tell apart, Janey often thought, the resemblance between brother and sister uncanny.

Both possessed the golden blonde hair of their Northern European ancestors and vivid but stormy blue eyes. They were two peas in a pod and together, a firestorm of sass of which Janey found charming.

Their parents were constantly trying to tame the wild spirit in the younger Epp, however, hence the reason for her chaperoned walks to and from school every day.

"If you didn't find yourself in trouble at every turn, Eva, I expect *Dat* would be much more lenient in allowing you to walk home alone," Jacob replied wryly.

"I am never alone!" Eva protested, crossing her arms about her cloak in defiance. "David walks with me!"

Both Jacob and Janey laughed aloud, casting the unassuming younger boy a glance.

"The day David Byler keeps you from trouble, sister, is the day I sell the family farm to the English and run for Hollywood to become an actor."

The elders laughed while the children sulked.

"I can keep us from trouble," David grumbled, speaking for the first time since leaving the school yard. "But I don't need to; Eva can take care of herself!"

Janey swallowed a whoop of laughter and gently pulled her small brother close.

"Yes, she can," she agreed. "The Epps are blessed with incredible strength."

Jacob shot her a look as they continued back toward their farms and she beamed.

They are a wonderful family, Janey thought, half-listening as the children carried on their ineffective protest. *When Jacob marries, I pity the woman who will have to contend with Eva for his heart.*

Janey groaned inwardly.

I need to worry less about the woman Jacob marries and more about the man I must find by Christmas. I only have one month.

Dinner had been filling and delicious.

"Thank you, *Mammi*," Jacob told his mother respectfully. "After the chill in the air today, that lamb stew warmed me to my gullet."

Fannie Epp smiled kindly at her oldest son.

"Some days I think you are the only one who appreciates my hard work, Jacob," she said jokingly, eyeing her husband who seemed half-asleep in his chair. Tom Epp did not stir nor acknowledge the gentle jibe at his wife's hand.

"That is not true, *Mammi*," Jacob assured her. "We all appreciate your hard work."

They exchanged a small beam and she nodded to show she was only jesting.

"After we have finished with the supper dishes, Jacob, I would like to talk to you."

Jacob's head jerked up slightly in surprise.

"Is everything well?" he asked worriedly. It was not characteristic of his parents to take him aside for anything. The Epps were a very open family without secrets or guile. If his mother wished to speak with him alone, it could only imply that it was something she did not wish his sisters to hear. Or his father.

"Do not seem so troubled, Jacob," Fannie replied. "I only wish to give you something privately."

"I hope it is a walloping!" Eva piped up from her spot.

"Eva!" their parents chorused but Eva returned to her stew as if no one had spoken.

"I would think you are the closest one to a walloping in this house," Jacob retorted and Eva stuck her tongue out at him.

"Eva! Mind your manners and finish your supper. You are holding up the table as always."

Skulking, Eva pushed her bowl aside and folded her arms across her chest, bowing her head so the strings from her prayer cap hung like lace in her golden halo of hair.

"I'm done!" she growled.

"*Gut*. You may tend to the dishes then," Fannie announced, rising from her spot at the table. She wiped her hands on her apron before gesturing for Jacob to follow.

"*Mammi*!" Eva protested. "I cannot do this alone!"

She shot Jacob a sly look as if she had won a battle but Fannie was well schooled in the way of her youngest's ways.

"Sarah will help you," Fannie replied without turning. She disappeared into the hall, leaving her daughters staring after her. The younger Epps quickly turned their ire toward Jacob but he averted their gazes and followed his mother into the small study under the staircase.

"I can help them, *Mammi*," he offered as he walked inside but Fannie shook her head, closing the door behind them.

"I need them to be occupied while we speak," she told her only son. "You know how willful our Eva can be when told to stay put."

Jacob did not need to argue. He was aware of the stubborn streak his little sister possessed.

"Sit down, Jacob," Fannie encouraged. "I wish to do this quickly before she comes wandering."

Jacob obeyed and stared up at his mother from the wing chair imploringly.

She moved to shuffle some books aside, reaching in to withdraw an item wrapped in a thick blanket.

"Now Jacob, before you speak one word, I wish for you to hear mine. Do you agree?"

"Of course, *Mammi*. I will not interrupt."

Fannie beamed, placing the bulging package on the table between them.

"You are such a good boy, Jacob. You are the pride and joy of your father and me. We have many blessings but we count you very high in the fold."

Jacob felt a slow blush rise to his cheeks and he looked down in embarrassment.

"That said, *liebchen,* you are just as willful and stubborn as your sister Eva."

Stunned by the backhanded compliment, Jacob opened his mouth to respond but Fannie shook her head.

"You promised to allow me to finish," she reminded him gently. "I will not be long."

Slowly, Jacob closed his mouth, watching as his mother began to unfold the blanket on the table.

"Your father gave this to me when he asked for my hand in marriage," she told him softly, withdrawing a beautifully crafted wood clock. "It has been hiding in the depth of a hope chest I have begun for Sarah and Eva."

She paused to hand the lovely piece to her son and he took it gingerly. It was a glorious product which someone had put many hours of effort creating.

"It is beautiful, *Mammi* but I don't – "Jacob started to say but his mother cut him off.

"I am not giving this to the girls," Fannie interrupted. "I am bequeathing it to you."

Jacob stared at her uncomprehendingly.

Oh, dear Gotte, is she ill? Is something happening to her or Dat? Am I to be responsible for the girls?

A thousand terrifying thoughts crossed through his mind as he stared at his beloved mother.

"*Mammi*?" he choked. "Why?"

"I want you to give this as your engagement present. It has bestowed much goodness on this family and I believe it carries good fortune."

Jacob began to laugh.

"*Mammi,* I am not engaged – I am not courting anyone even! While I am touched that you would give this to my bride-to-be, whomever she may be, it is quite pre-emptive, is it not?"

Fannie looked at him for a long moment, her face an indiscernible expression and Jacob was not sure if she was angry or thinking of something to say.

Have I done something wrong? Should I simply have accepted this? It is a highly unorthodox thing to do – giving a son a present for his bride-to-be, especially one that was bestowed upon you by your own husband. It should go to the girls -

"You sincerely are not acting, are you?" Fannie finally breathed, drawing closer to her son to stare him square in the eyes. "You...you don't see it, do you?"

Consternation began to sweep through Jacob as he returned his mother's gaze.

What in Gotte's name is she talking about?

"*Mamm*, I – I don't understand," he stuttered. "What...what are you talking about?"

Fannie exhaled so deeply, Jacob marveled that she had any breath left in her body at all. She sat laboriously in the chair at his side and took his hand.

"Jacob, I would not simply give you something so valuable to me to give to any woman, particularly not one whom I have no ties to," his mother told him. "I have given this to you so you can propose to Jane Byler."

The words were so unexpected, Jacob did not react for a moment.

Suddenly, the study was filled with laughter which spilled into the hallway and down the main floor. He knew he was angering his mother but Jacob could not seem to stop the mirth which was exploding from within him.

Fannie stared at her son with a slightly cold expression on her face.

"When you have finished chortling, you can explain why this is so amusing," she told him frostily. It took Jacob a moment to compose himself.

"I am sorry, *Mammi*," he choked, wiping a tear from the corner of his eye. "But Janey? Come on now!"

"Why not Janey?" she demanded angrily. "That girl is like a daughter to your father and I, Jacob. She knows you as well as you could want any wife to know you and you are inseparable now!"

Jacob abruptly stopped laughing and rose to his feet.

"I believe you have answered your own question, *Mamm*. She is like a daughter to you. She is a sister to me."

He found himself swallowing the last words as if they were razor sharp rocks in his windpipe.

"I am sorry if you had high hopes for Janey and me but it will not amount to anything."

He did not wait for his mother to respond, pulling open the sliding door to allow himself out. He ran directly into Eva who stood staring up at him, a scowl on her impish face.

"Eva, it is rude to eavesdrop," he chided but there was little force in his voice. He only wished to escape to his room without speaking to another soul but Eva stood firmly in his way.

"You cannot marry Janey," she told her brother in her typical matter-of-fact way. Jacob stifled a sigh and gave her a weak smile.

"I don't think you need worry about that, Evie," he replied tiredly. She continued to study him with her bright blue eyes.

Finally, she stepped aside and allowed for him to pass.

"All right, Jacob but I am serious," she insisted, eyeing her mother who appeared in the doorway.

"And why can he not marry Janey?" Fannie demanded. Eva shrugged.

"Because if he does, I cannot marry David and everyone knows that David and I are going to be married one day. I won't allow for you to ruin it!"

Jacob glanced at his mother and shook his head.

I will leave Mamm to explain the intricacies of marriage to her, he decided, excusing himself as he headed up the stairs toward his bedroom, trying to ignore the painful pang in his heart.

You need not worry, Eva. Janey and I will not be married. She has made that more than clear for many years.

There was a gentle tug on her long braid and as Janey turned to look, Jacob ducked back, trying to stay out of the line of sight.

"I can see you, Jacob Epp!" she called angrily. "And I felt you tug on my hair!"

"It was not me!" he protested but he could not maintain a straight face.

"I caught you in the henhouse, Jacob!" Janey shrieked. "What do you have to say for yourself?"

Jacob smiled and skipped closer to her, turning his big blue eyes on her lovingly.

"I am just practicing for when we are older," he replied.

"When we are older?" Janey demanded as she continued to glower at him, her brown eyes bright with annoyance.

"Yes," Jacob replied. "When we are married, I will want to touch your hair often. It is only right that I start now."

Janey woke, a smile on her lips, wanting to cling to the idyllic feeling of the dream.

Was that a dream or was it a memory? Janey wondered as she reluctantly rose to greet the morning. The dream seemed like something Jacob would say. When they were children, he often teased her that they would marry.

When we were young and naïve, Janey chuckled to herself, descending the stairs to meet her family for breakfast. *It is incredible how much life can change for everyone in only a few years. David dotes on Eva now but soon they will realize they are almost kin.*

Her father already sat at the table and her mother, Judith could be seen fussing about in the kitchen.

"Good morning, Janey," John Byler greeted his daughter. "You have a very becoming smile on your face. Did you sleep well?"

Janey's grin widened and she nodded at her father.

"Yes, I had a very pleasant dream," she replied. "I – "

She stopped herself, inexplicably embarrassed to recount the dream to him...or anyone else.

It will only be misconstrued, she decided. *No need to darken a perfectly innocent memory.*

"*Daed*, I am happy to have caught you before you left to tend to the cows. I have a very important request to ask of you."

John raised a busy eyebrow over the wire rims of his glasses.

"Oh?"

"Yes..." Janey glanced furtively at her mother and then behind her back to ensure none of her siblings had materialized.

"I have decided that I must find a suitor by Christmas. I would like your help in finding one."

She waited expectantly for her announcement to register with her parents who exchanged nervous glances.

Their reactions disappointed her although she was not sure what she was expecting.

Perhaps more joy? They should be ecstatic that I have decided to settle down.

Yet they did not appear to be.

"Why?" Judith asked flatly, sighing. Janey was confused by the question.

"*Why?*" she echoed. "Why what, *Mamm*?"

"I believe what your mother is asking is, why have you put such a constraint upon yourself?" John shot his wife a quick look and Judith pursed her lips, turning back to the dishes.

Janey sat back heavily.

"I have been watching my friends marry and I do not wish to spend another Christmas without a companion."

"You have a companion," David interjected, walking into the kitchen, rubbing his dark eyes. "His name is Jacob."

"It is rude to interrupt when the adults are speaking, David," Janey chided but the boy did not seem bothered as he took his chair, adjusting his suspenders.

"*Daed*?" Janey implored. "Will you help me?"

John cleared his throat and again gazed at his wife before offering his middle child a quick nod.

"I will see what I can do."

A grin of relief lit Janey's face and she resisted the urge to throw her arms around his burly shoulders. John Byler was not a man who was overly fond of outward affection.

"*Danke, Daed*!" she cried but John held up his hand.

"I think it is best that we keep this amongst ourselves if we intend to seek suitors for you, Janey," he said but he was addressing the entire family, including Seth who had finally made it down from his room. "This information might hurt others."

Janey's brow furrowed in confusion.

"Hurt who?" she demanded and Judith grunted aloud.

"Fannie is correct. Delusional. The both!" she muttered but Janey was not minding her mother. Her eyes were focussed adoringly on her father.

Daed will ensure I receive my Christmas miracle this year, she thought happily.

"Are we in agreement then?" John demanded. "No one outside the family must know that Janey is actively seeking a husband."

There was a murmur of consensus although Janey did not fully understand the terms.

It does not make a difference. It will only be silent until I find my perfect mate.

His mother's words had been reverberating in his mind since the night she had tried to give him the clock.

You must forget about Janey, he told himself. *She does not think of your as anything more than a brother.*

But every time Jacob tried to think of another he might consider for courtship, he always found himself comparing her to Janey.

Her laugh is terribly grating. Janey's is more musical. It does not grate on my nerves.

Others were not pretty enough or witty enough. There were ones who were too stern or not overly intelligent.

None of them is Janey Byler. And yet Janey Byler does not want me.

It was a terrible circle in which Jacob's mind raced but there did not seem to be an end in sight.

Until the morning the letter arrived.

"*Mamm*, what is this?" he asked, seeing the envelope in the kitchen. It bore only his name and address in an unfamiliar pen.

Fannie looked up from where she was making bread for their evening meal.

"I believe that is your father's way of pushing you to marry," she replied in her half-joking manner. "He spoke to Bishop Lewis about your inability to find a proper girl in the district so I do believe he has branched out for you."

"*Mamm*!" Jacob replied, aghast. "Why would you do such a thing?"

"I had little to do with it," she replied. "I told your father that you will run off any woman who attempts to write you the same way you do the women in this district but what harm can it do?"

Jacob stared at his mother, wondering if he had become so impossible to please.

He did not respond and instead took a seat at the counter near his mother, slowly opening the letter.

Fannie eyed him with interest as her son scanned the words on the page.

"Oh, come now, Jacob. You must read it aloud."

A red stain touched his cheeks and he glanced at her shyly but he did not know why. There was nothing in the letter which his mother could not hear.

"Dear Jacob," he started. "Forgive me for being so forward but my father suggested I might instigate contact with you. I have been told that we have much in common. I admit, I am somewhat cynical about meeting in such a fashion but I would very much like to make a connection with someone with similar interests. If I have not been too brazen in my approach, I hope to learn more of you also. It would be wonderful to make a new friend. Yours Truly, Jennifer Lapp."

Fannie chuckled lightly, her hands skillfully kneading the dough.

"What is amusing?" Jacob asked but his mother shrugged her shoulders.

"She sounds quite a bit like you," Fannie said, a small smile touching her lips. "Are you simply going to burn the letter then and forget it ever came for you?"

Jacob was not sure what he was going to do.

"There is not even a return address on it. How am I to respond?" he demanded, already making excuses for why he could not answer. Fannie made a noise which Jacob was unsure how to decipher.

"I am certain your father brought it along from the bishop. If you are looking for a reason not to write this girl, do not use that as it," his mother retorted and Jacob was immediately shamed.

"You know me very well, *Mamm*," he whispered and Fannie laughed aloud this time, shaking her head.

"You are my only son, Jacob. Of course I know you. I likely know you better than you know yourself."

Jacob did not doubt it and he rose from the stool to leave the kitchen.

"Where are you going?" she called to his retreating form. Jacob did not turn for he did not want his mother to see how pink his ears had become.

"To write Jennifer Lapp."

He pretended he did not hear his mother giggle.

There was an excited undercurrent in the air, one which seemed to flow from Janey to Jacob and back again.

He continues to look at me strangely, Janey thought as Jacob cast her another glance. *Yet he seems as jittery as me. Or is it merely that I am sensing my own giddiness. I do not know how much more I can keep this inside.*

The urge to blurt out the entire story was irresistible but Janey remembered the promise she had made to her parents.

Still, it did not make matters any easier. Jacob had always been her confidant. He should be the first one to know that she was in love.

That is ridiculous! Janey chided herself. *How can I be in love with a man whom I have never met?*

Yet, she knew it was so. She had never been so excited in her life at the thought of another man.

In his letters, Joseph Miller was everything she had ever wanted in another person.

He lived two districts to the east and Janey's father had assured her that the man was a good, solid man from a good family.

"I have met him numerous times," John Byler told his daughter and the words eased Janey's concern.

She dared not ask if he was handsome but she was yearning to know.

Janey would not admit it to anyone but when she read Joseph's letters, she had envisioned him to look like Jacob. There was much resemblance between Jacob and Joseph in his writing and speaking. He seemed even to enjoy many of the same things as her neighbor and best friend.

You should not think of him like that, she warned herself. *Or you will liken Joseph to a friend as you do Jacob.*

Yet she could not help but imagine Joseph to be a strapping blonde, blue eyed man with a dimple in his cheek.

Sometimes when I read his letters, I feel like Jacob is whispering them in my ear, she thought and while it had piqued her suspicion momentarily, she would have recognized Jacob's handwriting anywhere. They had been joined at the hip since they were babes in arms.

That day, as Janey joined Jacob on their daily walk to pick up the youngest, she felt as if she was a pot bubbling over with excitement.

Her only concern was that it was so near to Christmas and she had yet to meet Joseph face to face. She had brought up the subject several times but he seemed to circumvent it always.

He does not want to make the trip unnecessarily, she realized but it still was a stab to her heart. She was certain they would get along famously.

"You are very quiet today," Jacob commented. The snow was fresh and slippery and Janey used it to her advantage.

"I am simply trying not to lose my footing," she told him. To her surprise, he offered his arm.

"At one time, you would not hesitate to take my arm and bring me to the floor with you," he reminded her. Hesitantly, Janey accepted, flashing him a quick smile.

"At one time, I would happily have thrown you in the mud also," she agreed. "But much has changed."

"Has it?"

There was a wistful note in Jacob's voice and suddenly a pang of worry coursed through her as a realization struck her.

What if Joseph does become my husband? Will I move to his district or will he come here?

She looked at Jacob, a lump forming in her throat.

In either case, will I ever have the relationship with Jacob which we share now?

The answer terrified her and for the first time since the letters had begun arriving, Janey had second thoughts about meeting Joseph Miller.

If Janey was smitten with Joseph Miller, Jacob was half in love with Jennifer Lapp.

He recognized so much of his neighbor in what Jennifer wrote and like Janey, Jacob had been skeptical about the similarities.

Yet he also knew that Janey would never play such a cruel joke. He knew her handwriting after all.

Dat and the bishop simply know me very well. They found someone who was like Janey and sent her to me. I should be grateful that Jennifer and I have connected so well.

Yet when Jennifer broached the subject of meeting, Jacob was reluctant for reasons he did not understand.

He discussed it with his mother as they prepared for a feast with the neighbors.

"She would like for us to meet, Mamm," Jacob told Fannie that afternoon. "I am not certain I am ready."

Fannie Epp offered him her customary half-smile and wiped her hands on her apron.

"Why do you have your reservations?" she asked, gesturing for Jacob to sit at the table with her.

It was the night before Christmas Eve and the Epps were expecting four families in a short while yet Fannie did not seem concerned, barking orders at Sarah and Eva who pattered around the kitchen obediently.

"I don't know," Jacob answered honestly as Eva glared hatefully at him from behind his mother's back.

"Well you must look into your heart and ask yourself the reason you are holding off this meeting, Jacob. Is it fear that she will not meet up to your standards?"

"He is in love with Janey Byler," Eva grumbled. "This does not take a great deal of soul searching!"

"Eva!" Fannie and Jacob yelled in unison. "Mind your own business!"

Eva's scowl deepened.

"It is my business if he foils my wedding plans to David Byler!"

"You are a child, Eva. This is not a talk for now and this conversation is not about you!"

"It is always about Jacob," Eva whined. "Isn't it, Sarah? They never talk about us!"

As always, Sarah was quiet but Fannie laughed and shook her head.

"*Gotte* help us all when she is old enough to court," Fannie mumbled, trying to return her attention back to Jacob but the moment for seriousness had passed and Eva had not finished unleashing her fury.

"David Byler loves me just as I am!" the eleven-year-old asserted. "Unlike Jacob, he has no issue with expressing his feelings toward me!"

Noticing the pale in Jacob's face, Fannie whipped her head around to glower at her youngest daughter.

"You are a small child who has no knowledge of adult relationships. You will rue the day you spoke to your brother this way," Fannie told Eva. "You must not throw stones when you live in a glass house, Eva."

"I know plenty!" Eva shrieked again and Jacob shook his head.

"Yes, yes, David Byler loves you," he sighed. "I understand."

Eva's face grew scarlet as her eyes traveled toward the doorway. Jacob and Fannie followed her gaze to where the Bylers stood in the threshold, a bemused expression on their faces.

All but David who seemed mortified.

"David!" Eva cried as the boy turned to run from the room. Furiously, the little girl clenched her fists and screamed out.

"Your Jennifer wouldn't want to meet you anyway! You are doing her a great service by not meeting her no matter how much she grovels. Or maybe she is so pathetic, she will. Who else discloses so much personal information to man she has never met unless she is desperate?"

A dark silence fell over the kitchen and Jacob suddenly felt as if the room was spinning about him.

"Eva! To your room this instant!" Fannie raged, her face as white as the linens on the dining room table. Eva stomped her foot in anger and disappeared through the back steps onto the second floor.

Jacob could not look up but he heard Janey speak.

"What is she talking about?"

No one spoke for a long pause until Jacob looked up, his eyes shrouded in shame.

"It is nothing, Janey. I – I have been writing to a woman in a neighboring district," he confessed, shrugging his shoulders. "Eva may have a point about our relationship, however."

Janey slowly walked into the kitchen and looked at him closely.

"You have been writing to a woman?" she asked softly. "For how long?"

Jacob raised his shoulders again and then peered up at his mother who suddenly would not meet his eye.

"Three weeks, *Mamm*?"

Fannie did not answer but Jacob noticed that the color was slipping from Janey's cheeks, her eyes darting about the room as if trying to make sense of what she had learned.

"Do you have the letters, Jacob?"

He looked up at her, shame flooding through him.

"Janey, I do not want you to read them," he told her honestly but Janey shook her head.

"Go and get them," she insisted from between clenched teeth. "Unless you want to say something."

The latter statement was for her family who stood frozen in place looking uncomfortably about.

"I don't understand," Jacob said, looking from person to person but the stricken look in Janey's eyes was beginning to concern him.

"Janey?"

She stared at her father, her expression naked with sorrow.

"Why did you do this?" she demanded and Jacob could see her beginning to shake. "How did you do this?"

"Janey, we did it for you and Jacob," John pleaded. "You must not be angry."

"How?" she cried again. "How did you manage this horrible feat? Having us write to one another. You rewrote the letters so we would not recognize the handwriting and changed the signatures?"

"It was easy," Seth volunteered, leaning up against the frame of the kitchen as if he was proud. The oldest Byler sibling did not seem concerned in the least.

"Easy?" Janey gasped. "How can you say that?"

"Janey, you went to *Dat* to find you a suitor. He only put you together because you two are too blind and stupid to do it for yourselves," her older brother explained, toying with his suspenders. "If you had only opened your eyes for two true moments..."

"Fannie?" Janey gasped, turning to Jacob's mother. "How could you allow for this to happen?"

Suddenly, a wash of hot and cold coursed simultaneously through Jacob's body as he realized that his own mother had played a role in a deception which should have been transparent from the start.

And yet it wasn't...why not?

"Jacob, please forgive me but Seth is right. You and Janey have been made for each other since the day you were born. It never occurred to any of us that you would not feel that way when the time came. This little trick, all it did was prove what you already knew you had for each other. What harm was done?"

Jacob considered the question carefully and stared at Janey. His mother was right, at least in his mind. He had always known that he was in love with Janey but she was the one who had held back.

Had his letters swayed her?

He thought of the glow she had seemed to carry over the weeks and he knew that whomever she had believed she was writing over the past weeks was someone she had considered a romantic interest, not a brother.

"Janey?" he asked her and she looked at him, helplessly. "Are you well?"

She shook her head and sat in the chair which Fannie had been occupying and buried her face in her hands.

"How could I have been so foolish?" she cried, throwing her head back and staring at the players again. Once more everyone hung their heads in shame but her coffee colored eyes rested on Jacob and she shook her head, a tear falling from her eye into her cheek.

"How could I have been so blind when you have been here the whole time?" she whispered, leaping to her feet. "I am so sorry, Jacob. Will you ever forgive me for almost letting you go?"

Jacob leaned forward to wipe away her tear and smiled warmly.

"I would never have let you go," he assured her.

The room seemed to exhale in unison.

"Do not get too comfortable," Janey snapped at the others. "There will be a time of reckoning for what you have done."

A low, nervous chuckle filled the room before John piped up.

"But, liebchen, you asked for a suitor by Christmas and we have presented you with one, have we not?"

Janey sighed heavily and laughed weakly.

"I suppose all is forgiven then," she agreed. "Now that I have my Christmas miracle."

THE SHY AMISH MAN
SAMANTHA COLLIER

Rebecca's eyelids were drooping. Then the yawn came, long and low.

Mrs Helmuth, sitting to her left, started choking on her coffee. "Rebecca Beiler!"

But she couldn't help it. She had been up since five this morning, in preparation for her little sister's wedding day. It was four o'clock in the afternoon now, and the force of her eyelids was almost too much.

"Your *kapps* is eschew, Rebecca," Mrs Helmuth continued. The woman's eyes raked over her, assessing every imperfect detail. Why, oh why, had she drawn the short straw and been seated next to the district matchmaker and gossip?

Yes, her prayer cap had slipped. Stray dark curls were escaping from it. Her black dress, ironed hastily this morning, was now as wrinkled as Mrs Helmuth's face. But she wasn't the only one showing signs of wear.

Annie, the bride herself, was smiling fixedly. Levi, her new husband, was sweating as if it was a scorching summer's day, rather than a chilly one in late November. Rebecca could see their hands intertwined beneath the table, though.

Celery stalks, the traditional Amish wedding decoration, were wilting in their vases. The last of the season's brown autumn leaves fluttered onto the tables, and a bitter wind was whipping napkins into the air. The salads were drooping in their bowls. The hog in the middle of the wedding table was shrivelled. Children whined, clinging to their parents.

Hours to go, before she could make her excuses, leave the tables under the trees and climb the stairs to her room. There was still singing and storytelling after the banquet ended.

At least the wedding was at their own farm. Rebecca offered up a silent prayer: Thank you, Lord, for small mercies.

Mrs Helmuth heaved. She sounded like an out of tune piano accordion when she spoke. The whole table shook as she leaned across it, grabbing Rebecca's hand in her short pudgy one.

"A very busy day, my *lieb*. It is hard, is it not, seeing your little sister married, while you still occupy a single room in your parent's house?"

Rebecca flinched as if she had been slapped. Stop it, she said to herself. She doesn't mean it in a nasty way. She is just concerned that I will never marry. It is normal. It is the way of things. Oh, Lord, please give me the strength to endure it.

"Oh my dear, I didn't mean to distress you," Mrs Helmuth said, patting Rebecca's hand. "It just makes me so sad to see such a lovely and humble girl like you with no husband of her own. And I am here to change that for you!"

"What do you mean?" Rebecca couldn't quite keep the thread of alarm out of her voice.

"I mean, my dear, that I have made it my mission to find you a husband!"

"Oh, Mrs Helmuth, I appreciate it, but..."

"No buts, my dear. I have it all sorted. I have arranged a date with a young man for this Saturday night!"

Rebecca felt her face redden. Why was Mrs Helmuth doing this to her? Didn't she realise that she would rather walk over hot coals than go on a blind date? This had to stop!

"Mrs Helmuth, thank you, but I couldn't possibly..."

Mrs Helmuth raised an imperious hand. "I won't hear another word. My promise to you is this: by this time next year, you will have a good husband, just like your sisters!"

There was nothing Rebecca could do. And she didn't notice the pointed look that passed between Mrs Helmuth and her mother, who were locking eyes across the souring sauerkraut.

"Excuse me." The hot sting of tears was pricking behind her eyes.

As soon as her bedroom door closed, she threw herself across her bed and the tears came like molten lava.

What a terrible promise to make to a girl in her position! If only Mrs Helmuth knew the secrets buried in her heart. She could date all the men in the world, but she still wouldn't find the husband that she wanted. There was only one man for her.

And he wasn't here. She had looked all afternoon, strained her neck every time someone new had come, shuddered at the sound of boots on the hallway steps. Every yellow haired man had made her look again. All to no avail. She should have known. He rarely came to social events.

She had known him forever, as you knew everyone in her close Amish community. She had gone to school with him; she had attended church services with him; she had participated in Evening Sings with him, back when she was a teenager.

She had not seen him much during *rumspringa*, when the young people 'ran around', before making the decision to be baptized into the church and hopefully remain forever in the community. She had heard that he had gone away, and there were rumours he might not return. But he had. He was as much a part of their community as she was now.

Samuel.

Even saying his name, in the privacy of her own bedroom, under her breath, caused her to shiver. Then there was her joy at seeing the old worn green and white sign to his shop: Fisher's Bakery. The jingle of the bell as the door opened, and let her inside. The sound of his laughter from the back of the store, as he baked. Flour on the shop bench. Heat spreading from the ovens to the shopfront. She would crane her neck to see out the back, and always failed. But she knew he was there.

Afterwards, the explosion of sugar on her tongue while biting into one of his sugar cookies. Her favorite.

She sniffled into her pillow. She let her mind drift back to that one special day many years ago, when he had spoken to her...

It always dawned rosy on Apple Butter Day. The milk from the cows tasted sweeter. The cheese had extra bite. Even the eggs were yellower than normal.

Apple Butter Day had been a tradition in their community forever. It was like a holiday, and something that Rebecca looked forward to every year. It was held at a different community member's house each year, and that year it had been her families turn.

The neighbours gathered, and everyone started peeling the mountain of apples for the butter. Children ran in and out of the kitchen, laughing, their mothers shooing them away. The huge copper kettle had been brought out and set up over the wood fire. They had all taken turns stirring that huge kettle, to make sure that the butter didn't stick.

Samuel had come in for a glass of water. She hadn't noticed him behind her at the water pump. When she did, she flushed and glanced down, in shyness but also in demut (humility). She had expected him to take a glass and start pumping water. But he hadn't.

She looked up at him.

He was staring at her. The pale blue of his eyes looked like sky on a clear summers morning.

Then he spoke.

"For lo, the winter is past, the rain has come and gone," he said.

Then he poured his water and left.

Why was that memory haunting her now?

She had not known what he meant when he had said it to her. Was it a farming reference? Her studies had led her to the Song of Solomon, where she had found the quote nestled in amongst other words of beauty and wisdom. But still – what was he referring to?

Why couldn't she let it go? Why did it stay with her?

Sometimes she dreamed that she would walk into his bakery, and ask him outright. "One sugar cookie, please, and what did you mean about the rain coming and going?"

But she never did. The memory was fading slightly, like an old photograph yellowing with age.

He never even acknowledged her, any more.

She could hear footsteps on the stairs leading to her room. It would be her mother, or one of her sisters, come to fetch her back to the wedding. Telling her she had to stop being so sensitive. That she had to stop running away. What they had been telling her forever.

Taking a deep breath, she stood up and left the room, hastily wiping away the tears with the back of her hand.

***

"Rebecca! Keep still!"

The stool wobbled beneath her bare feet. Her mother had already stuck two pins into her as she hemmed her best dress. Saturday night was here, and her date was about to arrive.

"I don't want to go."

"You are going, my girl." Pins in mouth, her mother's voice sounded muffled. "Even if I have to drag you there myself."

"I don't want to date. I don't even know who this David Graber is! He isn't from our district."

Mrs Beiler pulled at the dress. "He moved here a year ago. To help his poor uncle with the carpentry after the heart attack." She pulled at the dress again. "Oh dear. I hope this dress length passes the *Ordnung* rule. I might have hemmed it a bit high."

Rebecca's dark eyes flashed. "It isn't seemly for me to be seen with a man at Shauffer's Restaurant. Especially in a dress that is too short. People will talk!"

"My, my, what a prissy little miss you are." Her mother was squinting at the needle in her hand, attempting to re-thread the last bit of cotton. "Lots of young couples go to Shauffer's now. It is perfectly respectable. You sound like an old Amish *grossmammi*! Do you want to just buggy date?"

"Nothing wrong with buggy dating," Rebecca huffed. "A thermos of hot cocoa, some sugar cookies...sounds perfectly lovely!"

"Are you twenty-two or sixty-two?"

Rebecca snorted. It seemed to come out of her nose like steam.

She tried a different tack. "The weather is turning. There will be a snowstorm tonight!"

"Rebecca, there is nothing wrong with dating," her mother said. "Both your sisters are married now! I worry about you, my girl. You need to socialize more."

"I go to the Evening Sings!"

"You do not. You haven't been in over a year. You sit at home with me making quilts, that is all!"

"But..."

"*Nein.*" Mrs Beiler was firm. "Hop down from that stool, your dress is ready. Go and put your *kapps* on, get your bonnet and cape and go and wait for him in the front parlour. You are going on this date even if I have to drag you there myself!"

***

Stop it, Rebecca said to herself. *Stop comparing them.*

But she couldn't help it. David's fingers were short and stubby, with a large amount of hair on them. Samuel's were long and beautiful – hadn't she watched them knead bread a million times when she had gone into his bakery? David's ginger hair was thin and receding slightly, while Samuel's was plentiful, and the colour of the corn in the fields on a bright summer's day. She didn't much care for David's table manners, either. He was scoffing his chicken pot pie like one of her father's pigs at the trough.

You concentrate on insignificant things, she scolded herself. *A man's character is more important than such vanity. Oh, Lord, please forgive this silly woman her pettiness.*

His pie smelt delectable, much better than the borscht she had ordered. But then, no one made borscht like her mother.

"How is your food?"

She looked up at him from her bowl, almost dropping the spoon in alarm. He wanted to talk!

"Fine, thank you."

An awkward silence. His ginger hair seemed to rise slightly from his head, as if it had been attacked by static electricity. She stared at him in distaste.

A figure loomed over their table. The waitress, of course, coming to ask them if they wanted dessert. Not if she could help it.

Except it wasn't the waitress. It was Samuel.

She flushed, turning the colour, she imagined, of one of the beets in her mother's vegetable garden. And her mouth was dryer than the sandpaper in her father's work shed.

"David," Samuel said, standing over the table. "I've been meaning to talk to you about your order of the pies for Christmas."

Samuel hadn't so much as glanced in Rebecca's direction.

"*Jah*, Samuel, could I pick it up on the twenty-second?" David responded.

"We are a bit understaffed now," Samuel said, then turned slightly and saw Rebecca.

He stopped, staring. The moment stretched on.

David watched them. "*Jah*, and is the twenty-second not good then?" No response. "Samuel? Do you know Rebecca?"

Samuel nodded, as if trying to dislodge a troublesome thought.

"*Jah*, Rebecca and I went to school together. I haven't spoken to her since we attended the Apple Butter Day two years ago."

Why was he talking about her as if she wasn't there? Rebecca wondered. It was probably just as well - she couldn't have trusted herself to speak. She was trembling like an autumn leaf about to fall from the tree.

David continued to look bewildered. "*Jah*, well, apple butter making is always good," he replied slowly. "About the order -?"

Samuel started.

"*Jah*, as I was saying, we are understaffed now and are snowed under. Literally!" he laughed, gesturing to the pale flakes swirling to the ground outside. "Could we possibly push it back to Christmas Eve?"

David nodded. "If it helps you, it shouldn't be a problem."

Samuel smiled. It was the first smile she had seen on his face since he had walked through the door. Samuel smiling was like a beam of sunshine breaking through a cloud on an overcast day. It made her want to bask in the warmth of it.

"Thank you, David," he said. "So much appreciated!" He paused, glancing at Rebecca.

"I shouldn't be disturbing your meal. I should go now."

Turning suddenly, he knocked the pepper shaker on the edge of the table. He grabbed for it at the same moment as Rebecca, who reached out her hand to save it tumbling to the floor.

Their hands touched.

Samuel gasped, his eyes narrowing.

He put his black felt hat back on his head and strode out of the restaurant.

David's mouth dropped open.

"What was that all about? That Samuel Fisher is an odd fellow, that's for sure. I remember talk that he lost his way during *rumspringa* and many expected that he wouldn't get baptized. I wonder if that contact with the outside world accounts for his strangeness?"

Rebecca was silent.

"Yes, well, we should probably get you home before the worst of this snow sets in. Ready to leave?"

More than ready. Her hand felt like it had been electrocuted.

She could barely stop it from shaking.

I have never felt anything like this in my life, she thought. *Pity Samuel hates me.*

***

The notes from the hymn rose to the top of the barn and hovered there like minnows in flight.

It was one of Rebecca's favourite hymns, and in that moment, nothing else existed.

She sang with all her heart. A song of joy and praise for our Lord. Time seemed suspended. In these moments, she felt as close to God as she ever could be.

Why had she stopped attending the Evening Sings? How could she have forgotten this special communion with God?

The final notes of the hymn stretched out, then ended. The boys and girls leaned across the table to each other. The sound of chatter filled the air.

It was always like this at the Evening Sings. The girls, in their church going frocks, at one side of the table. The boys, in their Sunday best, on the other. It was a different atmosphere to the service that had taken place here earlier. For a start, the hymns chosen were always livelier than the ones at the service. Rebecca loved the old, solemn hymns sang at the service – *Lob Lied* and *Amazing Grace* always brought a tear to her eye. But the Evening Sing hymns affected her differently. They made her want to shout out her love for the Lord to the world!

In between the hymns, the boys and girls would chat. And at the end, everyone would socialize for another hour or two. Often, a boy would take a girl home in his buggy. It was how the Amish courted. Rebecca had been to many as a teenager, as all Amish teenagers did. But she never chatted with any of the boys, and so never had anyone suggesting a ride home in his buggy to her. She hadn't minded. Her heart was always full of Samuel.

But he had rarely attended the Evening Sings, and hadn't spoken to her when he had.

It had been a long time since she had been to one herself. They were for teenagers. And she was an aging spinster, letting life and love slip her by.

The lovely euphoria the hymn had left her with punctured like a tack in a bicycle tire. She shouldn't have come. It was only at the insistence of Mrs Helmuth that she had.

The matchmaker had visited after the date with David, of course. "Well, my *lieb*, how did it go?" she had asked, as she settled at their kitchen table with a slice of her mother's apple pie and a coffee. Rebecca and her mother were putting the final touches to some quilts they were making.

"Terrible," Rebecca replied.

Why sugar coat it? The encounter with Samuel had ousted David completely from her mind. She had returned home that night convinced Samuel hated her. Why else would he have reacted the way he did when their hands touched, as if the slightest contact with her revolted him? And then to leave without saying goodbye.

Mrs Helmuth had coughed. "*Jah*, well, I have spoken to David," she said. "He seems to think that you are not a good match. He said he could barely get a word out of you. Rebecca, you have to try harder if you are ever going to get a fine husband and have a beautiful *bobbeli* of your own!"

"Well, maybe I am happy being here with my mother," Rebecca replied, a touch defiantly, then instantly regretted it.

Her mother raised an eyebrow at her over the quilt she was hemming. "Rebecca, remember respect."

"I am sorry, Mrs Helmuth." She felt her face burning as she looked down at her own quilt.

Mrs Helmuth's arms jiggled as she set down her coffee cup. "I do this for your own good. Remember my promise to you? Anyway, there are finer fish in the sea than have ever been caught. We will put David Graber behind us. This time you are going out with Timothy King. You know Timothy – the tall man who works at the dairy?"

She knew Timothy, and had never much liked him. And after another painful date, she had no desire to see Timothy ever again.

Next, Mrs Helmuth had pressured her into attending the Evening Sing.

"You haven't been for a while. It is time."

And so here she was. Mainly because her mother and father had left her behind after the service.

The next hymn started up, but Rebecca's heart wasn't in it anymore.

Her mouth moving but her mind distracted, Rebecca felt a fission of awareness. Someone was watching her.

Turning her head slightly to the far end of the table, she jumped. Samuel was sitting there, singing, but staring straight at her. When had he slipped into the barn? He surely hadn't been there when they had begun.

Their eyes met and locked. For Rebecca, it felt like everyone else in the room had melted away, and it was just the two of them, singing to our Lord and staring at each other.

Then it dissolved. He looked away, and the voices of all the others came back into her consciousness.

With a mumbled apology, Rebecca stood up quickly and left the barn. It was a dark, moonless night and she couldn't see her hand in front of her. Snowflakes drifted and fell upon her, cooling her skin. She raised a hand to feel her forehead. What was wrong with her? Was she getting a fever?

"Rebecca."

She turned to see a figure silhouetted against the gaslight of the open barn door. Was it him?

"My name is Eli Lapp, Rebecca. Is everything alright? You left the barn so quickly."

It wasn't him.

Rebecca forced a smile. "*Jah*, I just needed some fresh air," she replied. Disappointment pierced her heart.

Eli smiled. He was a tall, thin man with slightly bulging eyes. He held out his hand to her.

"I was going to introduce myself to you at the end of the night," he said. "Mrs Helmuth spoke to my mother about you, and suggested I talk to you. But if you are feeling a bit unwell, perhaps I might suggest I take you home now?"

Rebecca's heart sank. Mrs Helmuth. Of course. But she couldn't go back into that barn, and he was offering a way out.

"*Jah*, you are very kind," she replied.

She let him take her hand and lead her to his buggy.

As he helped her getting up, Rebecca didn't see that another figure had come to the barn door and was watching them. Nor, in the dark of the night as they trotted away, did she see that figure stay there watching. And kept watching, until the buggy was a tiny dot on the snow covered plain.

***

There was something magical about the lead up to Christmas, Rebecca always thought.

With only a few weeks to go, she was helping her mother with the Christmas baking. It was something that she and her sisters had done since she was small, and Rebecca looked forward to it every year.

Today the smell of almond cookies baking was permeating the air, and she was preparing a batch of walnut kisses to put into the wood oven. Her mother was stirring the mixture for sand tarts in a big ceramic bowl. Tomorrow they would bake pfeffermusse and Belsinckle Christmas cookies.

The snow had intensified, blanketing the farm in a thick layer of white. Rebecca almost sank into it when she had to go outside to do her daily chores, including milking Amelia, their docile cow. The weather was forcing passive activities on them. Mostly they quilted.

"Pass the milk jug, please Rebecca," Mrs Beiler asked, pausing in her stirring. Rebecca complied.

"So." Her mother wiped her hands on her apron. "Is Eli taking you out tomorrow night?"

Rebecca stopped what she was doing. "*Jah*."

Mrs Beiler shot her a piercing look. "You don't seem happy about that. Is Eli a good man?"

Rebecca shrugged. "Good enough, I suppose. He has bad breath, though, and – and – he pulls his fingers so the joints pop." She shuddered.

Her mother rolled her eyes and put down her spoon.

"Rebecca, there is something I want to say to you." She paused, as if choosing her next words with care. "You know that I love having you here with me. Since your brothers and sisters have married, it is wonderful to still have one of my children at home. It will be lonely when it is just your father and I rattling around this big house."

"You know I love being with you, Mamm."

"Yes, I know that my *lieb*." She reached out and patted Rebecca's hand. "But I must not be selfish. God does not smile on selfish women. I worry about you. You have always been my little lamb, hanging back. The others tore through life, full of confidence and bravado! Maybe I have over indulged you. You were always so timid, hiding behind my apron. But it has to stop."

Rebecca stopped cutting out the dough, and turned to her mother. "What do you mean, Mamm?"

Mrs Beiler took a deep breath. "I mean, you have to get out and find yourself a husband, Rebecca. You must try to be more social. That is why I spoke to Mrs Helmuth..."

Rebecca stared. "You were the one that set Mrs Helmuth up to harass me with dates!"

"Well, yes, but only for your own good..."

Rebecca didn't hear her mother. She had already walked away, climbing the stairs to the familiar comfort of her room. She tried to stop the tears from falling.

It wasn't that she didn't understand why her mother had approached Mrs Helmuth on her behalf. It was her duty to guide her daughter through life, and part of that was fielding courtships.

It was more that she felt disappointed in herself. She was failing as a dutiful daughter. She was a burden on her aging parents. She was a cripple. An emotional cripple.

She was disappointed that she could think only of Samuel. It was how it had always been, and why she had never gone on dates or pursued other boys.

But all that had to change. She was building her life on a foundation of tissue paper. Samuel had never expressed any interest in her. Granted, she had never given him much opportunity. Her love for him was based on one enigmatic comment from years ago.

The pepper shaker incident on her disastrous date with David showed that Samuel not interested in the slightest. In fact, he actively disliked her. He was revolted at her touch.

In need, she picked up her treasured Bible on her bedside table. Her rock, her comfort, her guide through life. Help me, Lord, she thought as she opened it. The beautiful words of 1 Corinthians 13: 11 confronted her:

When I was a child, I spoke as a child, I understood as a child, I thought as a child: but when I became a man, I put away childish things...

I put away childish things.

Closing the good book softly, she knew what she must do.

***

"Eli! Slow down! I am getting scared."

Rebecca was travelling with Eli in his buggy on an isolated country road. They were on the way to Rebecca's home after a date at Stauffer's in town. The night was as black as ink. Snow was falling in increasing intensity, and the ice on the road was making the wheels of the buggy slip and slide. Rebecca gripped the seat, trying not to lurch from side to side as the buggy swayed.

Eli was intent on what he was doing. "What did you say? I can't hear you in this wind."

Suddenly she was in the air, tumbling toward the embankment. Then all was still.

She awoke to the sound of horses whinnying pitifully. What happened? Where was she?

Stumbling, she attempted to claw her way back up the embankment. She could see nothing.

Then it all came rushing back into her mind.

We must have had an accident. Where is Eli?

She found her footing and managed to get to higher ground. The buggy was lying on its side; one wheel at a distance from it, still spinning. It must have come off, causing the accident. She couldn't see Eli anywhere.

"Rebecca! Are you hurt?"

Where did the voice come from? She didn't understand anything that was happening. Then she saw. A second buggy was further away, and a man was approaching her. Her brain didn't seem to want to work. I am having the strangest dream. I am on the side of the road, in the dark. I have had an accident. Samuel is here.

Samuel is here?

Yes, it was true. The figure approaching her was Samuel. Her heart filled with gladness to see him.

He was in front of her now, his face creased in concern. Then it changed to horror.

"You have blood all over you!"

Puzzled, Rebecca did nothing but stare at him. What was he talking about? She looked down at herself. Blood stained her best dress. She hadn't even known.

"Sit down, quickly, and I will have a look." Samuel held out his hand to assist her.

They found a spot by the side of the road. Rebecca sat down gingerly. "May I?" he asked, as he bent to lift her skirt. Rebecca shook her head. "*Nein!*"

"Rebecca, I have to see what's happened. We must stop the bleeding. There is no time for this."

With a pained sigh, she complied. The bleeding was coming from a large gash on her left leg. Samuel looked around. "Your cape. Pass it to me." He spoke softly but firmly. "And take off your shoe and stockings."

She took it off. He grabbed it, then ripped it in half, then again. Eventually he had a bandage he could use.

She was shivering now. The air was cold on her exposed leg. Samuel gently raised it, tying the ripped piece of cape around the wound. Snowflakes fell on her exposed skin, but his hands were warm.

"Stay there. Keep that leg raised." He looked around, finding a rock which he gently eased under her foot to keep the leg up. "Now, who were you with? You weren't driving the buggy alone at this time of night, were you?"

Rebecca shook her head. "*Nein.* I was travelling with Eli Lapp. I don't know where he is." She looked around, seeing nothing in the black of the night. He squatted beside her, putting an arm around her shoulders.

"It's alright. I will find him. Stay here."

He got up and walked away, calling Eli's name.

She drifted off. Next thing she knew, he was beside her.

"Now, Rebecca, listen. I have found Eli. He is on the other side of the road. He is drifting in and out of consciousness, and has a large bump on his head. I am going to put him in the back of my buggy, then I will come back and help you to it. Do you understand?"

Rebecca nodded. Her leg was beginning to throb.

After what seemed like an eternity, he returned and gently helped her to her feet. "Eli is in the back. Put your arm around me. Try to keep off that leg as much as possible."

She hobbled to his buggy, his arm around her. It felt natural, and good. It was ridiculous that she was thinking of that after all that had happened. Poor Eli was lying in the back of the buggy, moaning.

Samuel settled her next to him, putting his coat around her shoulders. And then they were on their way, driving past the wreckage of Eli's buggy.

"So what happened?" Samuel's voice interrupted her reverie.

When Rebecca finally found her voice, it sounded small and croaky. "The wheel came off."

Samuel looked at her sideways. "I know that. I mean, what caused it?"

Rebecca glanced at the still figure in the back. Eli appeared to be asleep. "I really don't know. The road is very icy."

"Yes, it is," Samuel agreed. "Which is why I am driving so slowly." He looked at her again. "How fast was Eli going?"

Rebecca reddened. "I don't remember."

Samuel didn't respond. They travelled for a while in an uncomfortable silence.

"So how long have you been seeing him?"

She jumped. She had been starting to drift off again. "I don't know. We have had maybe three dates." What did he care?

"Right." Did she hear a note of frustration? "Are you serious?"

Rebecca turned. "Not that is any of your business, Samuel Fisher, but yes. We agreed that we would announce our engagement after Christmas." A slight exaggeration, but he wasn't to know any different. I have put away childish things, she thought sadly as she spoke. That includes you, Samuel.

The buggy slowed down. Rebecca was puzzled. "Why are we stopping?"

He stared straight ahead. The horses nickered, stomping their feet a little.

"Do you think that is wise? You hardly know the fellow." He wouldn't look at her.

She turned to him. "I will say it again. It really is none of your business."

His face twisted then, with an emotion she couldn't name. "I am only looking out for you, Rebecca. You shouldn't be hasty, when it comes to such an important decision."

"Yes, well, the decision is mine to make." She was appalled to hear that her voice was shaking. "I am twenty-two years of age, a burden to my parents. It is right and good that I should find a man to marry and start a family of my own."

"Twenty-two?" He was frowning. "Well, you are more ancient than Methuselah! You will be needing a walking stick soon, I dare say." She looked at him sharply. Was he teasing her? But his face was impassive.

She drew herself up a little. "Please drive on."

He smiled. "Yes, of course, madam." And on they went.

She awoke with a start. The buggy was stopping again, this time at the front of a farmhouse that she recognized. And then she realised that she was slumped up against Samuel. She must have fallen against him when she fell asleep.

She sat upright hastily, pulling at her dress as she did so. "Where are we?"

He was jumping down from the buggy. "At old Dr Shetters. It's the nearest place I could think of to get you to for help."

A light had come on in the house, and a figure was coming down the drive holding a lantern as he spoke. It was Dr Shetter himself, who had been the district doctor for the community for over fifty years and had only recently retired. Dr Shetter had delivered Rebecca and all her brothers and sisters. He was a much-loved pillar of the community.

"Greetings! What have we here?" asked the doctor as he approached.

Samuel walked up to him. "Greetings, Dr Shetter, and apologies for disturbing you at night," he said. "I have brought you Rebecca Beiler and Eli Lapp, who have had a buggy accident. Eli is in and out of consciousness, and Rebecca has a deep gash on her left leg."

The doctor was assessing both as Samuel spoke. "Right then, Samuel, if you could help carrying Eli into the surgery. Rebecca, wait here, we will be back for you."

Half an hour later, Rebecca was sitting in a cosy armchair near the hearth in the living room. She was nursing a hot cocoa that Mrs Shetter had made for her. Her leg had been stitched and bandaged expertly by the doctor, and was now raised on an ottoman. The doctor and Samuel were still in the surgery with Eli, who appeared to have gained consciousness.

The doctor and Samuel walked into the living room.

"Rebecca, Samuel has just been to the telephone shanty and called your parents," the doctor said to her. The *Ordnung* rule was that members must not have telephones in their houses. Instead, there was a wooden shanty with a telephone which they shared, located at a central point between properties. "They will be here to pick you up in half an hour."

"You're not taking me home?" The words flew out of her mouth before she could stop them. She could have kicked herself.

Samuel looked at her. "I'm afraid I must get going, in the opposite direction to your place."

She bit her lip. "Of course. Thank you so much for your help tonight, I don't know what we would have done without you."

His face was impassive. "It was my duty by the grace of our Lord," was his reply. Then he picked up his hat. He looked around at all of them. "Goodnight, then." He turned to go, then glanced at Rebecca. "And congratulations for your forthcoming engagement."

Rebecca felt her face burn brightly. "Oh, Samuel, that is too hasty..."

But he was already off, and old Mrs Shetter, who was a lovely lady, but well known as a rival to Mrs Helmuth as the district gossip, had swooped upon her. Demanding what on earth Samuel was talking about.

***

".... And so it was, that, while they were there, the days were accomplished that she should be delivered. And she brought forth her firstborn son, and wrapped him in swaddling clothes, and laid him in a manger; because there was no room for them in the inn...."

Mr Belier's voice was strong as he read the Christmas Story from the Gospel of Luke to his family on Christmas morning.

Rebecca was spellbound, as she always was. It was her favorite story in the world. She loved this Christmas tradition of her father reading from the family Bible, while the family gathered around him.

Today, her little nieces and nephews were sitting on the rug. Her father sat in his favorite armchair. The rest of the family were either sitting or standing as they liked. Candles illuminated the windows. Cut out stars and angels were hung on string above the fireplace, where a huge fire was roaring.

"And there were in the same country shepherds abiding in the field, keeping watch over their flock by night. And, lo, the angel of the Lord came upon them, and the glory of the Lord shone round about them: and they were sore afraid...."

Rebecca smiled. She knew the story by heart.

" And the angel said unto them, Fear not: for, behold, I bring you good tidings of great joy, which shall be to all people. For unto you is born this day in the city of David a Saviour, which is Christ the Lord."

A lump had formed in her throat now, and she tried hard to keep back tears. Such a moving story.

She looked out the window of the living room to the first morning light glistening on the snow. She could see the Nativity scene that had been constructed the previous week. The children had made the display. Carved from wood, it stood out against a painted background. It looked spectacular against the white of the snow. She could see the figure of Mary, bending over the manger. How must Mary have felt, giving birth to our Lord in a stable, having to lay him in a manger? The humility of the Lord's birth place made tears spring anew in her eyes.

Everyone was getting up from their seats now the story was over. There were still morning chores to do. Horses had to be fed, the pig sty raked out, eggs collected from the hen house. She alone stayed sitting as everyone moved off, feeling useless and frustrated.

It had been two weeks since the accident, and Dr Shetter still wouldn't let her resume her daily activities, even though her stitches had been taken out and she no longer needed help to walk. It was good in some ways. She had been spared going to sing carols at the local aged care centre, which always made her nervous.

"Patience, Rebecca," her mother told her, when she expressed her displeasure at her immobility. "It won't be forever. Thank the Lord that you were not injured more seriously. Think of poor Eli, still bedridden."

How could she do anything but think of poor Eli? Since Samuel had told of their impending engagement to the Shetters, word had of course spread. She had had numerous visitors during her convalescence. They wanted to ask about the accident, of course, but seemed more eager to hear details of her supposed forthcoming engagement.

She blushed at their inquiries. "Please, don't speak of it. There is nothing to speak of! Eli and I were dating, that is all." How she hated speaking of such personal things to acquaintances! How she resented Samuel for putting her in such a position.

Samuel. She had not seen him since he had rescued them. He hadn't even bothered to inquire how she was doing. She didn't care anymore; she knew now that she was over her infatuation with him. Thank the Lord. It was better this way, much better...

She didn't think about Eli. She knew that as soon as she had the doctors' orders that she could leave the house, she should visit him. Maybe after Old Christmas....maybe.

Everyone was coming back into the house after chores, ready to open their presents. The children were whirling around in excitement.

There was no Christmas tree, and the presents were simple, in keeping with their customs. Each person had drawn a name out of a hat, and made or bought a present only for them. Rebecca had picked her older brother Aaron, and watched now in anticipation as he opened his present from her.

"Thank you, Rebecca," her brother said, as he unwrapped the hand knitted scarf. "Perfect for this freezing weather!"

Rebecca's present was from her older sister, Miriam. She gasped when she opened the box. Inside was a beautiful pale blue china tea set. She looked at her sister, unable to speak.

"For your hope chest," Miriam said. Then added impishly: "I hear that you might be opening that chest once and for all soon, Rebecca!"

"Miriam! Such indelicacy," scolded their mother. Rebecca couldn't think of a word to say.

"It's not, Mamm," Miriam continued. "Everyone is talking about how Rebecca and Eli are going to announce their engagement after he is well. Isn't that right, Rebecca?"

Rebecca still couldn't find her voice. Answer yes or no, she thought to herself. But all she could do was sit there like the fool she was, blushing as always.

Mrs Beiler changed the subject. "So what is this we hear that young Samuel Fisher is selling his bakery and leaving the district?" she asked the assembled group.

Rebecca flinched. What?

Another of her brothers, Joseph, spoke. "It's true, apparently. Everyone knows he has been having trouble keeping up with his orders. He is away now, looking for a buyer."

I do not care, Rebecca told herself. I do not care!

"He's been gone ever since he helped Rebecca and Eli after the accident," Joseph continued. "No one expects him back before Old Christmas."

Looking down at the pale blue china tea set on her lap, Rebecca tried very hard not to weep.

In the afternoon, the children took their sleds outside. They had a great time careering down the hill, laughing. They would catapult themselves off, throwing snow at each other.

Watching them through the window from her sofa, Rebecca couldn't help but remember when she and her siblings had been the ones on the sleds. Such simple times. Sometimes she wished she could return to that simple time. All you had to think about was what fun you would have after your chores were finished.

I put away childish things.

She thought she was doing the right thing, encouraging Eli. She had let him hope that there was an engagement awaiting them. She always knew that she didn't love him, but she thought that love might grow in time. She needed to marry and start her own family, become independent of her parents. She thought she had resolved herself to this.

Why then was she so sad?

And Samuel. By all accounts, he had gone away, was selling up. What had happened to his business? The thought of never being able to go into Fisher's Bakery again and order a sugar cookie made her heart ache.

She had to put him behind her. There had never been anything between them, anyway. The most that they had spoken had been on the night of the accident, and that was only because he had been forced to converse with her.

She meant nothing to him. He was completely indifferent to her. No, it was worse than that – he disliked her. Let's not forget the pepper shaker incident at Stauffer's, she told herself.

Lord, she prayed, give me the courage to get over this man. And let me find the way to love another.

***

Today was her first outside walk since the accident.

Christmas Day had come and gone, but in Amish tradition, the extended family had stayed on. There had been lots of outside activities with the children. The whole family had joined them in building snowmen and having snowball fights. They were constantly on their sleds. And, one day, they had all gone ice skating at a local lake.

"Can I come today?" was her almost daily refrain. But everyone said no, that she had to keep resting her silly leg! It was so frustrating. Even though she knew that they were doing it out of love for her, she felt excluded.

So, today was extra special.

Miriam and Annie had gone a little way with her, before being called back to the house for various chores. Today was the Epiphany; or Old Christmas, as they called it. January 6th. As important as Christmas Day itself to the Amish, there would be a big feast and they all had to pitch in to help. She had shooed them away, saying she would be perfectly fine and wouldn't go far.

It was only a small white lie.

She had skirted the creek, and was now looking over the iced water. It was a beautiful day. A pale light was making the snow glisten. But she should have listened to them. She was beginning to tire, and there was nowhere that she could sit and rest in the thick snow.

She looked over the hill and could see a figure approaching: a tall man in black. Relief flooded through her. It was Joseph or Aaron, come to help her.

She started waving, and the figure saw her and started heading in her direction.

Her arm stopped waving and fell to her side. Confusion etched her features. It wasn't Joseph or Aaron. It wasn't her father. Nor was it Levi, Annie's husband, or Dan, who was Miriam's. This man was not part of her family.

This man was Samuel.

Was he lost? Why was he on their property?

He approached her slowly. He was wearing his black felt hat, which dimmed his yellow hair. White snowflakes glistened, then dissolved on his black coat.

"Greetings," he said. Then he stopped, two steps in front of her.

Rebecca drew her cape tighter around her, and thanked the Lord that she was wearing her bonnet, which concealed her face. Her heart had begun to race.

"Greetings, Samuel," she replied.

He didn't seem to be in any hurry to speak further, simply gazing over the meadow toward the house. Rebecca felt herself trembling. Oh, Lord, why is this so hard?

"Did you have a good Christmas?" she asked, just to break the silence. Inside, she wanted to scream.

He stared into her face.

"Good enough," he replied. "What about you and your family?"

"Lovely, thank you," she replied. "Are you selling your bakery?" She could have kicked herself once the words left her mouth. It was too direct.

"You've heard talk." He looked down at the snow-covered ground. "People gossip. No, I was never intending to sell. But I was worried about the business. I have been away, looking for a new baker to hire, that is all."

"Why are you here, Samuel?" she blurted.

"To see how you are, of course," he replied. "After the accident."

Suddenly, she couldn't stand any of it, anymore.

"Well, I am mending, as you can see," she replied tartly. "Are you satisfied? Will you leave me be now?"

She turned, and started walking away from him. He followed, grabbing her arm to still her.

"Are you mad with me?"

She ripped her arm away, her dark eyes blazing.

"Mad? Why should I be mad?"

"You are most definitely mad," he said. But his eyes were twinkling.

"Are you laughing at me?" She felt close to tears now.

"I would never laugh at you, Rebecca," he answered. He looked solemn. "I respect you far too much."

"Respect me?" she scoffed. "You don't even talk to me! You go out of your way to avoid me. You acted as though you had been poisoned when our hands accidently touched in Stauffer's!"

He took his hat off his head, and scratched it, looking down at the ground.

She burst into tears.

Straight away, his arms were around her, soothing her. She felt her tears drying on his hair. He was crooning, whispering soothing endearments to her.

She stilled. She had never been this close to a man, apart from her father and her brothers.

As if compelled, she turned her face up to him. Then couldn't look away.

The kiss when it came was slow and sweet. She had no idea a man's lips could be so soft.

It ended, and she stepped away, confused. Her first kiss.

"Rebecca, I am a stupid man," he said. "I came here today to try to talk to you about my feelings. But I have failed, as always. I know that you think that I dislike you, but it couldn't be further from the truth."

He took her hand, looking deep into her eyes. "I love you. I always have."

It felt like a dream. Was this happening? Would someone pinch her, and she would soon wake up? She thought she was standing on a hillside in the snow, and Samuel had just kissed her and told her he loved her.

"You love me?"

"Yes. With all of my heart."

"You love me," she repeated, in wonder.

"I knew that I loved you since that Apple Butter Day at your house, just before *rumspringa*. But once I realised, it was like I always knew. But I didn't know if you returned my feelings. You were always so shy! And I am like that, myself." He looked down at his feet.

"Oh, I know that people call me odd and say I am haughty, but really, it is because I don't know what to say or do around people most of the time. So, I keep to myself. I didn't know how to approach you. Every time you came into my bakery, I would look at you and long to speak to you. I would promise myself that next time you came in I would, but I always lost courage." He paused.

"And then I saw you dating a few men. When it became obvious that you were going on dates with Eli Lapp, I gave up, I am sorry to say. But I have been away and thought long and hard about it; I have prayed and prayed. The Lord has told me to approach you."

He took her hand.

"Rebecca, if you are serious about Eli then I will walk away from here today and never bother you again. Even though he is not much of a man! He did not take care of you properly that night. He was riding the horses too hard on the icy road. He caused your accident."

He glowered. "The thought of what could have happened to you has been tearing me apart!"

She looked up at him. He wanted to protect her. He said that he loved her! So, she forced herself to speak all that was in her heart.

"Samuel," she said. "I didn't want to date other men – it was my mother and Mrs Helmuth who made me! I have only ever wanted you. That is why I always came into your bakery."

"Not for my delicious sugar cookies?"

She laughed. "Your sugar cookies are delicious, but no, not just for them! But you never noticed me. I thought I was a silly woman, hoping where there was no hope. I needed to get married, so I thought maybe I could learn to love Eli. I tried! But it wasn't any good. I went to see him a few days ago and told him that I can't date him anymore."

He reached down and stroked a dark curl that had escaped her bonnet. "So you don't love Eli?"

She shook her head. Tears had sprung in her eyes again. "I love you," she said.

Suddenly, Samuel let out a holler and picked her up, whirling her around. "She loves me! She loves me!"

Rebecca burst out laughing. How could so much happiness be contained?

"I left Stauffer's that night, knowing for sure that you were my love," he said. "Brushing your hand was like coming home. It was like my body recognised yours." He shuddered.

"That is why I went to the Evening Sing. It was to see you again, and maybe approach you. I overheard Mrs Helmuth in the bakery, saying that you were going. But then Eli came to you..." His voice tapered off. He looked lost.

She couldn't bare it. She reached up to him and softly trailed her hand over his face. He turned to it, and kissed it softly.

"If only we knew," she whispered. They had loved each other, forever, but their shyness had kept them apart.

"Well, it is all good now," she smiled. "And maybe we can thank Mrs Helmuth for that."

He raised an eyebrow. "How so?"

"Well, if she hadn't forced me to go on dates with other men, you might never have got the courage to approach me." She looked at him shyly.

He grinned. "You could be right. We should thank her! She has done her job well – if only she knew it."

Rebecca looked around, and saw Aaron and Miriam in the distance, approaching them. They must have been drawn by Samuel's shouts.

"Others are coming," she whispered.

He drew himself up. "Shall we go and join them? I would like to come to your house and speak with your father, if I may." He looked down at her again. "Will you marry me?"

This couldn't be real. And yet it was. "I will," she breathed.

"Thank you, Lord," Samuel said. He turned his eyes to the sky, overcome with emotion.

They joined hands, then turned to face the others.

She stopped. "Samuel, what did you mean when you quoted the Song of Solomon? On Apple Butter Day."

He knew instantly what she meant. "I saw your face as I turned around. You were so beautiful! My heart was overflowing with the Lord's love." He paused. "I wanted to tell you that it was a new season, a new day." He blushed. "Maybe for us, by the grace of God."

"And so it is," she said. "By the grace of God."

Suddenly, it struck her: Mrs Helmuth had said she would have a fine husband within the year. A smile slowly spread across her face.

The matchmaker's promise had come true.

AMISH CREEK

MONICA MARKS

<u>**Winter**</u>

The night had taken on a cold chill and it was somehow fitting of the heaviness in Jacob's heart. He gently urged the horses forward as they shied from an oncoming car, carefully guiding them closer to the ditch at the side of the road. Ahead of his carriage were two more, one for each of his brothers and their respective wives. The family was approaching the market and Jacob was grateful for his hands were slowly freezing against the reins despite the heavy woolen gloves covering them. The three carts eased into the wide parking area to the left of the treeline and Eliza, Jacob's younger sister-in-law, was the first out of carriage, already busying herself with the merchandise in the back of the wagon. By the time Jacob pulled his horses to a full stop, she had managed to unload a substantial number of goods. She smiled briefly at him as he approached to assist her but waved him away.

"It's all right, Jacob, I am quite capable of handling this here. You can go about whatever you need to do in your carriage." Jacob nodded but said nothing. He had never been one to say much.

"That's why you're not married," Jonah would tease him. "The women have no idea what you're thinking. How are they supposed to know that you have marriage on your mind when you say so little?" Jonah had no way of knowing how his words upset Jacob as it was merely meant to be brotherly teasing but Jacob often wished that he was more outspoken. Yet when he was in the presence of his female peers, he found himself more tongue-tied than usual. Gabriel and Jonah often pointed out the blue painted gates of the eligible women in town but Jacob always averted his eyes and changed the subject or maintained complete silence. Eliza and Jonah had just wed the previous month and as his just barely younger brother hopped down to join his new wife, Jacob could not help but feel a pang of envy at the new scruff covering his sibling's face. Subconsciously, Jacob found himself touching his own clean shaven, soft cheek, wondering if he would ever be able to boast the beard of a married man.

"Come along now, Jacob," Gabriel urged suddenly appearing at his side. "The cheese will freeze if you stand here too long."

"Really, Jacob," Louisa scowled. "You know better than to stand there while our goods go bad." At the sound of his older sister-in-law's voice, Jacob shifted his eyes downward and picked up the pace of unpacking the freshly churned cheese onto the wheelbarrows Eliza had dug out from the depth of her cart. Louisa was the dark, complete opposite of Jonah's sweet natured, cheerful mate. Louisa was only a year older than Jacob but she looked and acted like Jacob's ninety-year-old grandmother. She was starch and rigid and unlike Jacob's beloved grandmother, never had a kind word to say. Jacob could never understand why his older brother, Gabriel had married such an embittered woman. Gabriel was without a doubt the most attractive and hardest working member of their family. He was mild mannered and intelligent and he could have had his pick of any number of eligible women in their community. However, that was neither here nor there at that moment as Louisa's look of anger was deepening by the second as she watched Jacob's idling. Gabriel took the wheelbarrow from Jacob's hands, also noticing the look on Louisa's face and followed Jonah and Eliza toward the indoor market, Jacob close behind them, Louisa on his heels like a rabid sheepdog trying to keep in in line. Once inside, Jacob was relieved for the wood burning stoves which were filled with fresh wood and already warming the giant barn, despite the early morning hour. Someone had taken care to ensure the vendors were comfortable upon their arrival. It was barely six o'clock and the winter sun had yet to break through the blackness of night but the smell of the wood against cold winter air brought a surge of familiar melancholy to Jacob. He had been feeling lost the past few months, as if he were missing a key element, like air or water. He suspected that Jonah's wedding had helped bring about the sudden loneliness. *You need to find a wife and start a family. You're twenty-five years old. You are the last man in the family and you're unmarried. Even your younger brother is married before you! That is shameful!* Louisa's sharp tone snapped him out of his brooding.

"Are you going to stand there until the sun goes down, Jacob?" He shuffled forward without looking up, joining the rest of his family at their booth. He liked this venue. It was a true Amish market, lit with soft gaslights and no electricity. It had once been an old, neglected barn belonging to a vast colonial house but years after the family who had owned it went bankrupt, the land was distributed among the Amish communities evenly. The house had been demolished and Jacob's family lived on one part of the fruitful farmland, raising goats, cows and chickens. They had been dairy farmers for generations. A neighboring district had reconstructed the dilapidated barn, expanding it to four times its size and they had created a small trader's market within the grand structure. Everyone was welcome, provided they respected the land. On any given day from Tuesday to Saturday, there were merchants selling jams and quilts, sweaters and meats. Only the freshest vegetables and cheeses could be found in the simple wooden booths, packed in ice and metal buckets. Once in a while, a more ambitious traveler would set up a crate boasting homemade wine or cider but those peddlers were becoming more and more scarce as the demand for their supply diminished. While it was open to the general public, it maintained the virtue in which Jacob was raised and he felt more at home at this particular location than any of the others at which they frequented over the year. Their cheeses were on display in a very short time and now there was little else to do but wait for traffic. Eliza immediately sat upon a skid of wood and began knitting while Louisa seemed content to stand back, arms folded and tight lipped, sternly watching the vendors prepare to the upcoming day.

"Did you bring something to read, Jacob?" Eliza asked brightly, smiling at him. Jacob nodded quickly and lowered his blue eyes, blushing. Her smile widened but she did not tease him. Jonah, however, seized the opportunity.

"We are ever so grateful that you did, Jacob! Otherwise you might never stop talking!" Jacob reached into his burlap sack to remove a book he had recently borrowed from the library in Lancaster, ignoring his brother.

"Leave him alone," Gabriel growled at Jonah. "At least he knows when to stay quiet."

"Oh, quiet yourself, Gabriel. If I can't tease Jacob, who can?"

"No one needs to bother Jacob," Eliza piped in pleasantly. "I think it's wonderful that he has such a disposition. It will take him far in life."

Jacob almost hugged his new sister. Instead he offered her a timid smile before looking back down at the pages before him.

"No one needs to be silent all the time," Louisa retorted. "Really, Jacob, how are you going to court anyone without learning how to speak?"

"That's enough!" Gabriel snapped. Everyone looked at him in surprise, including Jacob. "Jacob will marry when the time is right and he will speak to someone when he finds someone worthy of hearing his voice. Now leave him be!" Inexplicably, tears sprung into Jacob's eyes. Jonah looked abashed while Louisa looked contrite.

"Of course," Louisa mumbled, retreating to her spot against a post. Gabriel drew close to his younger brother.

"There is nothing wrong with you. You are patient, kind and you will make a just minister to our district one day. Don't let anyone tell you otherwise."

"Thank you, brother," Jacob murmured. Gabriel patted him reassuringly on the shoulder and went to join his wife. Jacob watched him walk away and wondered if that speech of confidence was actually for him or if Gabriel was just thinking to himself aloud.

The day got colder even as the sun fought to break through the ominous clouds. A storm was brewing and the market was suffering as a result. Only a few people had dared venture out as the temperatures dropped to a desolate, inconsolable place. It was the kind of day where even the marrow of the bones was chilled and could not be warmed under any circumstance. Most of the patrons were tourists passing through Amish country but a few neighboring communities stopped by to provide their support. Jacob was happy he had thought to bring along another book as he had barely had occasion to raise his eyes from the first one he had packed. Then fate mysteriously intervened.

It started as a shriek. Startled, Jacob looked up and blinked as an object came hurling at his head. Out of nowhere, a body slammed into his and he was belly down under the neighboring booth, Gabriel on top of him. A peal of child's laughter rang out, followed by a group chuckle and it was clear that whatever had occurred had merely been the act of a clumsy or mischievous child. But as Jacob rose put his hands down to raise his body up, his eyes locked upon a pair of light brown irises, crouched down like a preying tiger directly at his level. There was a face inches from his underneath the table, their lips almost touching one another. And suddenly Jacob was not in the din of the market any longer.

They skipped in a circle, the long grasses tickling their knees as the group picked up speed. The scent of wildflowers and herbs filled the air. Jacob's head was feeling light and he wasn't sure if it were as a result of the dizzying game or the beautiful eyes of his classmate, Grace which seemed to be fixated on his own. Even at the tender age of eight, Jacob recognized the impossible beauty of those orbs, a luminous, liquid brown, so light they seemed gold in the springtime sunlight. The round dance continued a few more laps until Grace herself "tripped" and landed the group into an unceremonious pile of young, panting bodies onto the lea. Yet through the reeds, Grace still stared at him and he at her. And not once did he feel the urge to look away in shyness.

"Jacob!" the eyes spoke. Quickly, Jacob lifted his head to stand and hit his skull against the booth, creating a sickening crack at the impact. His hand raised instinctively to his head.

"Oh! Are you all right?" She was at his side, grabbing his arm in aide. Jacob was immediately torn. He knew that he was not supposed to have this kind of contact with an outsider but this outsider was different...she was Grace.

"Uh...yes, thank you. Hello Grace," he mumbled, staring up at her. "How are you?"

Grace smiled that off-centered, charming grin which could disarm the angriest of bees.

"I'm well, Jacob. I'm so happy to see you here! I have been here a few times in the last months but you are never here when I come. I have been yearning for your goat cheese for years now and I finally had the courage to come around. Have you any for sale? Truly you can't find anything like your family's cheeses in the city."

Jacob nodded and before he could lead her around to the booth, he was looking up directly into Louisa's scowling face.

"Come along, Jacob," Louisa intervened, pulling him from Grace. "You're needed."

"But she wants – "Jacob protested.

"Eliza can help her," Louisa snapped. "Eliza! Help this woman!"

Louisa almost spat the word "woman" as she scathingly glared at Grace. Grace looked forlorn as she watched his sister-in-law shuffle him away. She slowly raised a gloved hand and smiled sadly as he looked back at her.

"Bye Jacob," she mouthed.

"You should know better, Jacob," Gabriel chided. They were back in their home, gathered by the warm hearth of the fire, counting their profits from the day. Jonah and Eliza looked up questioningly.

"Oh do tell! What could our patient Jacob possibly have done to earn trouble?" Eliza joked. "This I must hear!"

"Your brother-in-law was fraternizing with a fallen woman, a shunned member of this community," Louisa snapped. "Looking after her like some lost lamb. You should be ashamed of yourself, Jacob! You are just asking for trouble!"

"Who?" Eliza and Jonah chorused. "Which shunned woman?"

"That Beiler woman," Gabriel replied quietly. Eliza's eyes lit up.

"Lydia?" she squealed. "Oh how is she?"

Louisa's frown deepened into her characteristic scowl.

"No, the other one. Grace. Their poor, shamed parents. Can you imagine? Having two of your children living scandalously in the city? What are the odds of that occurring? It's no surprise they're in such poor health."

"Jacob, you saw Grace today?" Naomi, Jonah's twin looked up from kneading bread to address her younger brother. "How did she look? Is she well?"

Jacob nodded. Naomi and Grace had been very close before Grace had left the church. Naomi had been devastated when Grace had been exiled and she had never completely recovered. Probably no more than Jacob had.

"She said she was well," Jacob replied.

"You spoke to her?" their father was incensed from his rocking chair at the hearth. "Jacob, I expect better from you!"

"She was there to buy cheese!" Gabriel jumped in. "You cannot make a sale if you do not speak with the customers, papa."

Jacob looked gratefully at his brother.

"In the future, you let the women handle the women," their father muttered. All the siblings exchanged a secret smile, except, of course, Louisa.

"Jacob, what a pleasant surprise. How are you?" The bishop looked up from a pile of papers and smiled at the man in his doorway. "Please come in."

"Hello, Bishop. Is this an opportune time?"

"Of course! I don't get to see enough of you. Oh! Wait! I know what this is about! You're here to announce a betrothal!" The heavy set man clapped his hands together, his eyes lighting up with happiness. "Who is the lucky woman?"

Jacob shook his head quickly and averted his expressive blue eyes.

"No, Bishop. It's not a marriage announcement..." The bishop read Jacob's somber expression and his smile faded. He gestured at a simple chair across from his desk.

"Please sit down," he encouraged the younger man. Jacob obliged, still staring at the floor.

"Is something wrong, Jacob?"

"No...well..." Jacob paused, unsure of how to word what he wanted to say. He wished he had asked Gabriel for advice before doing something this inane. If his father found out...well it was too late now.

"Bishop, if someone were to be excommunicated, could they ever come back?" Sighing, Bishop Fisher sat back against the rigid chair and pushed his spectacles off the bridge of his nose, onto his receding hairline.

"Jacob, the idea behind rumspringa is for you to see what waits for you beyond the security of our community. That is why we look the other way when the young people go and experiment with different aspects of the world in which we don't engage before making the very important choice of being baptized. Once you are baptized, we expect that you have 'sowed your wild oats' so to speak. So Jacob, if you are having a crisis of faith, we can help you through community and prayer but if you choose to leave the Amish community now, it will be very difficult for you to return. Realistically, I would say nearly impossible. "

Jacob laughed, startling the man.

"I'm sorry, Bishop. I didn't mean to laugh. You needn't worry about me. I have no desire to go anywhere away from my family and land. I was asking about someone else." The bishop looked slightly more relaxed but curiosity gleamed in his eye.

"Could you give me the circumstances?" he asked. Jacob suddenly realized his mistake. The community was too close. There was no possible way that this meeting would not reach the ears of his family. He was acting like a foolish child, making this trip and asking ridiculous questions. Why would he assume that Grace would ever want to come back? She most likely loved her life in the city. She and may even be married already! Shame stained his cheeks crimson and Jacob stood suddenly.

"I'm sorry, Bishop. This was a silly thing for me to do. I made a mistake." Without waiting for an answer, Jacob hurried out of the small house and down the road toward his farm.

Jacob was about to vomit. He could feel the bile raising to his mouth, creating a pool of saliva under his tongue. *Don't get ill! You foolish, foolish man! What are you doing here?*

An elderly woman smiled kindly at him and handed him a paper bag from beside her seat.

"Motion sickness, honey?" she asked. Tentatively, Jacob accepted the bag. Then, to his horror, he retched into it. Surprisingly, after he was finished, he felt much better. The aging woman nodded knowingly.

"There you go. My grandson gets carsick too. He's only ten but I carry bags just in case. I didn't think people got carsick at your age," she told him.

"I've never been on a bus before," Jacob admitted. Her grinned widened and she nodded understandingly, taking in his simple, homespun clothing.

"Well that would explain it then. Just take deep breaths and try to relax. We'll be in Philadelphia in less than an hour." Jacob nodded and tried to heed her advice but his stomach would not settle. He imagined that had more to do with what he was doing than the actual bus ride itself. This was completely out of character for him. In fact, he could hardly believe what he was doing. He didn't know what he was hoping to accomplish but he also knew that since the day he had seen Grace in the market, he had been unable to think of anything but her. Her heart-warming smile was in the fireplace, her dark honey eyes were in the rays of sunlight streaking through the pines. He heard her voice in the chirping birds and once he thought he even saw her standing behind their barn but of course it had only been his mind playing tricks. He could not get her out of his head. He had to know if she was happy, if she thought of him or at least if she missed her life and her family in the district. Of course what he was doing was forbidden and if he were caught, he would be punished. But that would be the least of his problems. He would never hear the end of it from Louisa. Yet none of that seemed to matter. He would not rest until he knew that Grace was happy in her life. Even if that meant she was content without him.

As the older woman had predicted, less than an hour later, the bus was pulling into the hectic station in Philadelphia. Jacob had never seen such chaos. During rumspringa, he and Jonah had gone into town twice. Jonah had put on outsider clothing, smoked a cigarette and drank beer. Jacob had almost been sick from all of the foreign smells and the bustle. While he had accompanied his brother, he never felt the need to experiment with anything he did not know. There had never been any doubt that Jacob would be baptized. Unlike his peers, he had never felt the need go outside of is upbringing to see how good was their life. He recognized the purity in their way, the unity they had with nature and with each other. He couldn't imagine a life without the structural peace in which he had been reared. Jacob had always felt blessed by his birthright and respected the culture immensely. It was for all of these reasons that his underarms were soaked in perspiration at that moment, despite the crisp winter air. He nodded good-bye to his bus mate and slowly walked off the vehicle, his head swimming from all of the activity. *Stay focussed on your task, Jacob. You will be home before anyone realizes you are gone.* Once off the bus, he reached into the pocket of his plain brown pants and withdrew a scrap of paper. Then looking about, he spotted a taxi cab stop on the outskirts of the bustling station. Without hesitation, he made his way into a car and muttered the address written on the piece he was holding. The cabbie raised his eyebrow slightly at the sight of his passenger but made no comment at Jacob's outdated clothing.

"Is this your first time in Philly?" the man asked pleasantly, somehow feeling the need to put his obviously uncomfortable fare at ease. Jacob nodded quickly but stared out the window. His head was beginning to ache from all of the sights and sounds whizzing by the window.

"There's a lot of history here," the driver offered but when Jacob did not reply, he gave up and continued the relatively short trip to his destination. Jacob paid the charge and nodded before climbing onto the sidewalk. As the car drove away, he found himself looking back at the paper and then up at the apartment which he faced. He was in the right spot according to the phone book he had consulted at the Lancaster Library. This was Grace's home. For a moment, he considered aborting the mission all together and running back to the safety of Lancaster County. *But then you'll never know,* he told himself. And that was all the convincing he needed. He started up the steps and was inside the tiny entranceway, looking for her name on the intercom system. A teen boy walked out of the lobby and held the door open so Jacob slipped inside, rather than searching for the code. The phone book had declared Grace's apartment to be 401. Jacob opted for the stairs rather than the elevator. He reached the fourth floor and knocked on the door boasting 401 in scarred gold numbers. After a moment, he heard footsteps and a woman sing out.

"Coming!" Jacob swallowed and tried to prepare himself for coming face to face with the only woman who he had been able to speak with his entire life. But when the door flew open, it was not Grace. In Jacob's intense disappointment, he almost walked away, not realizing that he was looking at Lydia, Grace's younger sister.

"Jacob Miller! I don't believe my eyes!" she hollered. "Grace! You won't believe who is at our door!"

Jacob turned back to the doorway he was already departing, his eyes filled with hope at the sound of Grace's name.

"Is Grace here?" he asked, his voice no higher than a whisper. Lydia nodded eagerly and ushered him into the tiny apartment. Seconds later, Grace appeared in the hallway, her lava-like eyes wide with surprise.

"It really is you, Jacob! What – how...oh don't tell me you've been excommunicated!" Grace cried, rushing forward to embrace him in a hug. Not wanting to move but willing himself to do so, he stepped out of her friendly gesture and shook his head, color blushing his face with embarrassment.

"No...I...I came to see you, Grace," he said. "Is there any way we can speak? Just for a few moments?"

Lydia looked shocked but quickly nodded and said she was on her way out. She picked up a set of keys from the kitchen table and smiled briefly before flying out the door. Before she closed the door, she turned to Jacob, her eyes shiny.

"I understand that your brother wed Eliza Lapp. Please, if you find it in your heart, can you tell Eliza I think of her often?" Lydia did not wait for an answer and Jacob realized it was because she was about to cry. The door to the apartment closed and Grace smiled welcomingly at Jacob.

"Please, come and sit down. Can I offer you anything? A tea?" Jacob shook his head and sat down on the edge of an old velvet sofa.

"I can't tell you how wonderful it is to see you! I haven't been able to stop thinking about you since I saw you last week. I have been trying to find covert ways to see you and Naomi since I left. This has been my only fruitful attempt thus far. How is your sister?

Jacob nodded.

"She is well. She heard that I had seen you and asked the same. I believe she misses you very much, Grace." She smiled sadly.

"I miss her also. And I miss you, Jacob. You were my very first love." Jacob was stunned to hear the words. He had hoped, maybe even suspected that Grace had thought of him lovingly but he had always been far too bashful to find out if she held the same types of feelings for him. He felt like a weight had been lifted off his chest, a barbell which had resided upon him since the horrible day that Grace had left his life.

"Why don't you come back?" he asked her seriously. "Do you want to come back?"

Grace sat heavily back against the rocking chair in which she sat.

"Very much, Jacob but it is not that simple. If Lydia wanted to return, she would have a much easier time of it. She was never baptized so in theory, she never really left the church. She's basically on an extended rumspringa. I, on the other hand, have been baptized and I turned my back on my vows to our community."

"Why did you leave?" Jacob pressed before he could stop himself. He wasn't sure he wanted to hear the answer. He had always feared that she had fallen in love with an outsider. Grace's face fell.

"When Lydia began her rumspringa, it was just about a year after you and I had been baptized. Justine and Joseph had just gotten married and it was only Lydia and I left in the house with our parents. The workload doubled and I was fine with that but Lydia had always been willful. She began to act out and refuse to do the work. My parents' health had begun to fail at that point.

Suddenly, Lydia was not coming home at night and I would go looking for her and find her in cars with boys, high off marijuana, wearing skimpy clothing. I was only grateful my mother never had to witness anything of the sort or she would surely be dead by now of a heart attack. Night after night, I would drag Lydia home, pour cold water on her head and sober her up but this wasn't just a phase. I knew she was going to leave." Grace paused and looked up at Jacob.

"She is my little sister, Jacob. She is lost and naïve and doesn't know the ways of the world. She needed someone to protect her. She had no one..."

Jacob felt a lump grow in his throat. Grace was such an incredible sister. Would he do the same thing for Jonah or Naomi? He was ashamed but he knew that he would not. It took courage to do what she did for Lydia.

"How is Lydia doing now?" Jacob asked. He feared the answer.

"She is wonderful! She went to college and got a degree as a paralegal. She met a very nice man, a lawyer and I do believe he is going to propose any day now." Grace smiled but Jacob read the pain in her eyes.

"Do you want to come home?" Jacob asked again. Grace nodded slightly but changed her affirmative into a shrug.

"That's really not relevant, Jacob. I won't be welcomed back. I have learned to accept that fact. I knew what I was doing and this is my penance for making such a choice."

"You must speak to Bishop Fisher, Grace!" Jacob told her. She shook her head.

"You must go back home, Jacob and forget about me. If anyone finds out you were here..." She rose and went to guide him to the door.

"I can't tell you how wonderful it is to see you, Jacob. If you somehow find a way, tell your sister I miss her dearly. But don't put yourself into any trouble doing so." Instinctively, she reached out and embraced Jacob. Before he could stop himself, he had wrapped his own arms around her and relished the feeling of her closeness for one blissful moment. It might be the last time he ever had the opportunity.

"Good-bye, Jacob," she whispered in his ear and slowly closed the door, leaving him staring at it, troubled and confused.

"Bishop, is this an inopportune time?"

"Jacob! You left so quickly the other day, I thought it was something I had said!" the jovial man rose quickly from behind the scarred desk and hurried to greet Jacob at the door. "Please come in!"

Jacob moved further into the small office and sat before the elder, choosing his words carefully.

"Have you come to further discuss what we started the other day?" Jacob nodded.

"Sir, do you recall the Beiler sisters? Grace and Lydia?" The man frowned deeply, apparently troubled by the mention of their names.

"Yes," he replied slowly. "Why do you ask?"

"Grace would like to come home," Jacob answered simply. The Bishop began to shake his head at once but for the first time in his life, Jacob felt a rod of steel fuse into his spine and he sat up straight in his chair. He would not take no for an answer. Not this time.

"I do not think that is in the realm of possibility, son," the kindly man said. "Now if Lydia wanted to rejoin us, that might be possible since she has yet to be baptized however, it would be a process – "

"Lydia is very happy living in the outside world. Grace knows her place is here with us." The bishop continued to shake his head and Jacob felt his jaw clench, a motion that was foreign and unsettling to both men. Bishop Fisher seemed to recognize his anger at once and tried to diffuse the situation with logic.

"Jacob, what you are asking is out of the question. Grace Beiler chose to leave after she already committed herself to us. She not only abandoned our community, she left her own family to contend with an awful burden from both a labor and personal standpoint. Surely you cannot ignore those facts!" Jacob stared defiantly at Bishop Fisher.

"You don't know all of the facts, Bishop or you would change your mind," Jacob almost spat between clenched teeth. "Grace Beiler is an honorable woman and she belongs here with her people. She is willing to repent and undergo whatever punishment you deem fit to allow her back but please, Bishop, you must consider this!" Again, the Bishop shook his head, his eyes misty with sadness.

"This is not my decision to make, Jacob. Grace already made the decision for herself. There is nothing I can do. You must forget about Grace Beiler. There are many eligible women who would be very fortunate to be wed to you, Jacob. Please try to focus on what is feasible.

Grace Beiler is a dream." The Bishop stood up, indicating the conversation was done. Jacob felt familiar the lead weight of loneliness overwhelm his chest. He had known that this was apt to be the end result but he would have never forgiven himself if he had not given it a sincere chance. But he had failed. And Grace would never be there to untie his tongue as she had in childhood. As he slowly let himself outside into the cold winter afternoon, he somehow didn't see Grace's eyes in the sunlight for the first time since their encounter at the market.

<u>Spring</u>

The first day of warmth was a time for celebration among the Miller family. Although the temperatures had just barely climbed above freezing, it was enough to have melted the snow and cause a slushy mess for children to stomp around while the men bravely retired their heavy wool coats and the women dared leave the wash on the line all day without fear of freezing the handmade fabrics. Even Louisa seemed to be in a good mood as the brand new baby buds dripped snowflakes into puddles of water and caught the golden sunrays in their reflections. Louisa had just discovered she was with child and for the first time that anyone could remember, she was actually smiling. It was a lovely smile, in fact and quite infectious. In fact, she often had kind words to say. The only one unaffected by the magic the season change appeared to bring about was Jacob. Not even Jonah and Eliza had been able to lift him out of the depth of his despair since his meeting with the Bishop. Of course Jacob had not disclosed the reason for his mood but instead thrown himself into work. When he was forced to be in the presence of others, he ensured he had a plethora of reading material at his side as to avoid any potential conversation. The day that the warmth finally remembered their district, Jacob had been up well before dawn, milking the cows as he always did. He wanted to be done the majority of his chores before retreating to the barn and hiding in the loft. He had actually acquired an interesting mystery from the library and he was eager to read the ending. As the morning hour turned close to noon, Jacob hurried out of the chicken coop with a basket full of eggs and almost slipped in the mud near the pig pen. Steadying himself before he lost the day's yolks, he grabbed onto the fence with his free hand and looked up. Directly on the other side of the gate was the most beautiful woman he had ever seen. Her long blonde hair was loose and hanging about her gray, ankle-length dress, under a matching gray bonnet, slightly blowing in the gentle breeze. Her mouth was turned up into a crooked smile, off centered but intensely charming and as it always did, sunlight caught the molten brown of her eyes, melting the sadness out of Jacob from the moment his forlorn irises met them.

"Grace!" he whispered, hushed and looked around figuratively. "What are you doing here?"

Her beam widened.

"This is my home, Jacob, and I've come to thank you for helping me find my way back. And also I would like to inform you that my parents have painted their gate blue."

Late Winter

No one could have prepared her for the man standing on the other side of the door but it truly was Bishop Fisher and he was there to speak to her. Lydia had conveniently disappeared, extremely uncomfortable by the reminder of the past she had left behind but Grace had welcomed the Bishop into the cozy apartment, offering him a hot tea and they had talked for hours, about Lydia, about her parents, about why she had left and of course, about Jacob. After their discussion, the Bishop told her that he wanted to have her return but he needed to discuss it with the ministers first. Of course, the process would be long and require intense atonement for what she had done. There was one more subtlety; that she would sincerely consider Jacob as a husband. Grace had smiled and nodded. After he left, she had shaken her head and laughed. How could the Bishop know that the main reason she had wanted to return for so many years was to be with Jacob?

Amish Christmas : Sylvie's Gift

MEGHAN MASON

The Christmas Angel: Sylvie's Gift

The soft delicate flakes of winter's new snow fell gently upon the fields, as Thomas looked around at all that was left to him this year. This time three years ago, his beloved wife, Maddie, had died in childbirth. It was a traumatic and utterly devastating loss for Thomas and for his first-born daughter, Sylvie. Maddie's pregnancy had been fairly predictable, with the normal morning sickness, and odd food cravings here and there. However, when the time arrived for Maddie's labor, the village doctor had to be sent for. Maddie's labor had stalled, and the baby's head was stuck in the birth canal. By the time Doc Masterson arrived, there was little he was able to do to make Maddie more comfortable. Doc Masterson and his midwife worked well into the night, trying desperately to reposition the poor boppli's head to no avail. Maddie began to fade, as she could not push the baby without having contractions. By early morning, Doc Masterson came out to the kitchen,

"Thomas," he nodded for Thomas to remain seated. "Maddie and the boppli are gone. Neither made it through the very difficult and prolonged experience. With labor stalling out, and boppli's head not able to reach oxygen, there was just no way. It was a dear boy, Thomas. Go to Maddie..." and Thomas remembered nothing else the Doc had said. He was consumed by sadness and heartbreak. Maddie had been his true love, and he thought they would be together forever. Thomas could only weep as he held Maddie's limp, cold hand. He never noticed little four-year-old Sylvie, peaking through the crack in the doorway. Although Sylvie was far too young to understand the trials of childbirth, she did understand that mamm was not coming back. She cried behind her daed for a long time before Doc and the midwife noticed she was hiding behind the door.

Those memories seemed distant now, as Thomas held out his hand to catch a falling flake. However distant, Maddie would always remain in a special place tucked safely deep within his heart. He had worked so hard to gain control of his life for the sake of Sylvie. He had a daughter to provide for, and a home to keep in addition to the fields. It had been rough going until Thomas had hired on part-time help from the neighboring farmer's wife, who had three grown daughters of her own to lend out to needy families. Becka had been a blessing from Gott, but now Becka was off to marry and begin her own family. Sylvie was now seven years old, and was attending school. She was also learning at a very early age how to perform simple household chores. Though she was still relatively young, Sylvie learned fast, and wanted to please her daed by being a little home-maker. Though Sylvie's efforts were admirable, there was still much that Thomas had to do around the house after all day in the fields. He bore this responsibility with honor and grace, as he wanted nothing more than to provide Sylvie a wonderful life. He knew there was still something missing, and he knew that Sylvie longed for a mother's attentions. He did not know the answer, and supposed he was doing the right thing by serving as both mamm and daed to the girl.

Time had arrived for the Chrischdaag season. With the pretty snowflakes and family excitement felt at every farmhouse in the village, Thomas knew that Sylvie would be getting ready to perform at her school's annual sing-along. Every year, the schoolhouse would put up decorations of holly and ivy greens, sing songs, tell stories, read poems, and put on the traditional play to celebrate the true meaning of Chrischdaag (Christmas). The true meaning revolved around the glory of the birth of Christ, making this one of the most important religious observances of the Amish community. As Thomas reveled in his own private Chrischdaag memories, he heard the front door slam, and in came Sylvie,

"Daed! Daed! Guess what? I got a part in the play this year, and I get to play an engle (angel)! I am to wear a white dress and bonnet with a beautiful star in my hands. Miss Eddles says she'll loan me the costume from last year, as you don't know how to sew!" Sylvie exclaimed with joy, "I just love Miss Eddles!"

The next day at school, Sylvie tried on the pure white gown, and looked upon herself in the full-length mirror in Miss Eddles' office room. She imagined that she looked just like an engle! She thanked her teacher for the loan of the pretty dress, and couldn't help but wish somewhere deep inside her heart that the kind and good Miss Eddles, otherwise known as Annalise amongst the townsfolk, was somehow coming home with her at the end of the day. After all, Miss Eddles had all the markings of a beautiful and worthy mother, didn't she? And that is what filled Sylvie's thoughts and prayers from that point onward. In fact, Sylvie's wish was not so out of the realm of possibility, if she could just think up some clever way to get her daed and her teacher in the same room, away from all the other children. Sylvie decided the best thing to do right then was to confide her most special secret to her bosom friend, Diana. Sylvie and Diana had been best friends for as long as either of them could remember. At lunch, Sylvie called Diana over to the tree where they always sat,

"Diana! Over here! Let's not sit with the other girls today. I want to tell you a big secret! I was just thinking...wouldn't it be grand if my daed and Miss Eddles got married? Then my new mamm would be my favorite teacher," coaxed Sylvie.

"Oh yes! That would be perfect, but I don't see how that is ever going to happen," agreed her friend, "unless...we came up with a plan to have them meet somewhere, you know, like a surprise."

"That is impossible, Diana. We never go out anywhere, because daed is always busy with choring."

"But Sylvie, what about Christkindlmarkt? Aren't you going with your daed to do Christmas shopping, and visit the craft stalls? I go with my mamm and daed every season before the schoolhouse play!"

"That's a great idea, if only I could convince daed to take me too," complained Sylvie, "he always left me at home with Becka before. Now that Becka is gone, maybe I can come too. Then we can arrange a meeting between Miss Eddles and daed!" Miss Eddles began to ring the hand bell to signal that lunch was over, and it was time to get back to the classroom,

"Come on, let's go in, and tomorrow I'll tell you if daed will take me with him," coaxed Sylvie, and the two friends ran back to class.

Later that afternoon, once Sylvie had returned home from school, she was preparing the simple meal for their supper. The dinners had to be of a simplistic nature, since she was only seven. Thomas didn't mind plain meals, because by the time he finished choring in the fields, he was bone tired. He felt sorry that poor little Sylvie had to be the one to carry the load of household duties, but there was no other option. Thomas went to wash up, and returned to the table,

"This looks delicious, dear Sylvie," Thomas encouraged, "how was school today? Did you practice your part for the play?"

"Yes, daed, I tried on my dress too!" she cried with delight.

"Daed? This weekend is the Christkindlmarkt in the village center. Can we go together this year?" she implored her father, "I think I'm big enough to go too, and then I can help you with Chrischdaag preparations. Please, daed?"

"Well now, you are seven years old, and becoming quite the accomplished young woman of the house, so I guess that sounds alright. If we get all the choring done bright and early on Saturday, I don't see why you can't accompany me!" and Thomas gave Sylvie a big smile, as he felt proud of her efforts to be more mature than her years. Despite his pride in her however, he felt sorry that he couldn't be more to the girl. The years had made him tougher, but he still felt the pangs of loneliness. He longed for a wife that could keep him company and discuss the farm with. He missed the easy friendship he and Maddie had had in those early years when Sylvie was just a boppli. But Thomas was not one to show weakness or demonstrate feelings, so he stuffed those private pains deep down inside, careful not to betray a single thing wrong to his daughter. The last thing she needed was to feel sad for her ol' daed, or think she was not doing enough around the house. Thomas dove into the soup and declared with exaggerated gusto,

"My, my, Sylvie! This soup is marvelous! Best soup you've ever made! Let us thank Gott for our many blessings." And so, father and daughter ate their meal together, and talked occasionally of how they would decorate the house for the season of Christ,

"When we go to market this weekend," said Thomas, "we shall choose some modest greenery for the hearth. You may construct the garland for the very first time. Your mamm was usually the one to do that part, but you are ready now, I suppose." He paused at that remembrance, and his daughter could see the faraway look in his eyes. She knew that he missed Maddie so much. Maybe Miss Eddles could ease the pain of her father's loneliness, she thought. Then the task of garland making could be a mother/daughter activity. One that her daed would not dread remembering.

Thomas snapped out of his reverie, as he accidentally spilled soup over his trousers. Sylvie ran to fetch a cloth from the sink, and Thomas continued talking as if nothing had happened,

"Remember to bring the market basket when we go! It's best that we get there early right after choring. Then we must also select a wreath for the front door. It will be nice to have you there, Sylvie, to help pick one out this year. We can make stars out of the paper sacks that the oranges come in. That will spruce the place up for Chrischdaag."

The next morning at school, Sylvie set to work on thinking how to manage getting Miss Eddles and her father to run into one another at the Christkindlmarkt! There had to be a way to do it, so that she didn't look too responsible. She was so terribly desperate to bring her daed happiness this year. And she also felt that his happiness would in turn spill over into her own visions of having a real family again. Just then, she was broken from her lovely daydream by her teacher clearing her throat, and calling out Sylvie's name,

"Sylvie? Sylvie! You will not accomplish any arithmetic if you are not listening when it is your turn at the blackboard. Now is there something you'd like to share with the class that has you so preoccupied?" she asked with the slightest grin.

"Ummm, hmm, uh, I was just thinking about Christkindlmarkt this weekend. Will you be going, Miss Eddles?" she blurted out in front of the entire class. She could feel the heat rise to her cheeks, as her classmates chuckled,

"Yes, I will indeed be doing my season shopping this Saturday, however, I fail to see how that relates to the math problem on the board," and Miss Eddles handed her the piece of chalk, "Now up you go." Sylvie didn't mind the minor scolding in front of the class. Now she knew that they would all be in the same place on the same day! That's all that mattered to Sylvie. She proudly grasped the chalk, and walked confidently to front of the classroom to take her turn at math.

As the day wore on, it was finally time to be dismissed. Miss Eddles reminded everyone to bring their costumes on Sunday to the village center, where they would perform the annual play for the community and families. Sylvie could scarcely contain her excitement as she waited for the teacher to clang the dismissal bell, and she proceeded to run full speed all the way home. Tomorrow would be Saturday, and she planned on staying up a little later tonight so that she could get some of the morning chores done ahead of time. There was so much to be done, including planning the grocery list for the ingredients needed for the Chrischdaag dinner! She had been planning it for the last month, and wanted this to be the best and tastiest dinner she'd ever made! As soon as she walked in the front door, she set to work cleaning and cooking the supper. Then she gathered eggs from the hen house for morning, and baked bread and laid out the marmalade for the breakfast. Her final task was to make her shopping list in the secrecy of her bedroom. This way her daed would be completely surprised by the menu this year. She would make all the traditional fixings, such as roasted chicken, mashed potatoes and gravy, and cranberry stuffing. Her masterpieces would be the pumpkin bread and cherry pie that she had never attempted before. She would also remember to make her father's favorite holiday candy, peanut brittle and divinity fudge! He would never suspect that she had chanced upon her mother's old recipe box. It had been stuffed way back behind the sugar and flour sacks in the storage closet. It had been printed in her mamm's pretty script on a small card that she had marked, "Thomas' favorites." Sylvie's eyes began to droop, as she noticed the clock on her bedside table. It was far past her regular bedtime, and she knew it was going to be a very big day tomorrow. She quickly put her list in the pocket of her day apron, and changed into her nightdress. She undid her now messy bun, and brushed her hair the way she remembered her mamm doing when she was so little. Then off to sleep she fell, after lots of tossing and turning with excitement.

The air was chilly, and it looked like new snow would soon follow, probably by evening, so Thomas and Sylvie headed towards the village center for Christkindlmarkt. They could smell the aromas of the roasting chestnuts, fresh produce, pine and sweets. As they approached the first stall, she spotted Miss Eddles. She was standing on her own at the wreath booth. Sylvie tried hurrying her daed along, but he was far too interested in the various tools and farm equipment out for display. Sylvie watched on, as Miss Eddles moved on until she was out of sight. Her heart sank with disappointment. Father and daughter moved slowly from one stall to another, choosing bits and pieces for decorations and grocery items required for Christmas dinner. Sylvie took hold of the basket, and gave an excuse so she could shop for the special candy supplies. If her daed was not to meet the beautiful and charming Miss Eddles, then at least she could still focus her dreams on preparing old favorites for their puny family celebration. The snow began to fall as Thomas called out for Sylvie,

"Sylvie! We best start back towards home, or we'll get stuck in a snow storm. Did you find all that you needed?"

"Yes, I'm finished with my shopping, so let's head home," she answered with a heavy heart. Her plan had failed. She resolved to give up trying to be a match-maker for her father, and tried to concentrate all her efforts on the holiday meal that was going to take up much of her time, plus the schoolhouse performance tomorrow. She was so exhausted by the time they reached the farm, that she scarcely had the energy to prepare supper and finish her nightly chores,

"May I go to bed early?" she asked Thomas, and he could see how tired she looked from the day's activities.

"Why, yes, my dear. Go on to bed. You have another busy day tomorrow. The play would not be complete without the Christmas angel, so rest up," and he added that she could have the rare indulgence of sleeping in till well after sunrise. Thomas looked at his young daughter with some concern, as he felt she already did far too much for a girl of seven.

Sunday morning arrived with a fresh layer of pure white snow. As Sylvie awoke from a dreamless sleep, she realized that today was the day she was to play an angel. However, the disappointment of yesterday still stung, and she was not nearly as excited as she once had been about the performance. With a heavy heart, she clambered out of bed, dressed for her chores, and went to the kitchen. There sat her daed, eating his breakfast,

"Daed! Why are you eating alone? I would have happily made us our breakfast!"

"No, Sylvie, not today. This is your big debut in the schoolhouse play. I wanted you to sleep in for once, and not have to worry about tending to housework. You need to be a child occasionally, mostly because that is precisely what you are. I also took the liberty of completing your other morning duties. Consider it an early gift, because in a few days it will be Chrischdaag!"

Sylvie flung her arms around her father in a grateful and loving hug. Then, she hurried back to her room to prepare for the play. She couldn't help but admire the simple beauty of the white gown that her teacher had loaned her. She imagined that Miss Eddles had sewn it herself. The stitches were done in the finest embroidery thread of a slightly different white so that it stood out just enough to be seen. The tiny pattern swirled in an uncomplicated design, but one that looked like angelic halos. The bonnet was snowy white to match. Sylvie rehearsed her lines in her head while getting herself ready for the trip into town. Then, costume on under her heavy winter coat, she stopped to view herself in the mirror. She began to cry. No efforts to make her father less lonely or herself less lonely had worked. It was heartbreaking to imagine the rest of their lives just being the two of them. No mamm around for advice, comfort, or knowledge of how a girl's life should be or what kinds of things to expect. In that one moment of staring at her face in the dusty mirror, she fought the urge to rip off the gown and not attend the play. Angry with herself, she swiped at her tears, straightened her hair, and put on a cheerful face for Thomas,

"Alright. Let's go. I'm ready."

Her daed answered back, "the buggy is ready to go! Mind your shoes and the hem of the dress when you hop in. It would never do to have the angel arrive in tatters."

The trip into town was silent, with Thomas not understanding that Sylvie's desire not to speak was not simply stage fright. He eased the buggy into the parking area, where lots of other families were arriving with their children. Sylvie jumped out of the buggy,

"Bye! I'll see you after the performance, daed." She ran with the other kids headed towards the entrance of the schoolhouse. Thomas lingered by the buggy, making sure the ties were securely attached. What really held him back was his insecurity at attending the first school function all alone. Everyone knew the history, yet he felt that they were only speaking to him out of pity. He steeled himself to enter the noisy hallway and find a seat. He reminded himself that this was about his daughter rather than himself, and put all thoughts of uncomfortable situations to the back of his mind. He trudged through the snowy lane in his boots, not bothering to look up. It was then that he bumped into someone or something, and he fell to the ground, losing his hat and burying half of himself in the freshly fallen snow. Aghast, he looked around in the evening light, and saw that he had apparently walked straight into a young woman carrying loads of boxes and papers. She was face first in the snow, the contents of her boxes strewn around her in a mess. Thomas, humiliated, got to his feet, and swiftly tried to help the woman up. It was clear that she had sprained her ankle in the fall, and he felt embarrassed and completely responsible for his clumsiness. If only he had been watching where he was going,

"Oh, my goodness! Please, take my hand. It's entirely my own fault, as I was lost in my own thoughts! Are you hurt?" He extended his hand to the poor disheveled woman, her bonnet askew, and her dress torn at the hem,

"Thank you, and please, I was carrying so many things that I could hardly see two feet in front of me! I'm terribly sorry for the trouble, sir!" she exclaimed.

"No. Please, allow me," and Thomas began to gather the fallen items and place them all back into the boxes. He noticed that they were all decorations for something, and it suddenly dawned on him that this might be his daughter's teacher. He had never met her before since choring kept him home on the one parent night of the year. He realized this must be her, and felt a pang of guilt that he was most likely the only parent who had never shown up. It was not for lack of interest, but of having little to now time in the evenings to attend such functions,

"Forgive me, are you Miss Eddles, the school teacher?"

"Why, yes, I am, and I think the children will be worrying where I have gotten off to at this late hour. The performance is about to begin, and here I am slipping and sliding in the snow," she chuckled nervously, "Who are you, sir? I do not think we have met?"

"Oh, I am Thomas, Sylvie's father. I apologize for knocking you down. What can I do to help?"

"Just help me gather all these garlands that we appear to be tangled up in, and I'll be about my business getting the children ready," she stammered. She knew she was running dangerously late, and the children would be wondering what was going on,

"Please, call me Annalise. Annalise Eddles. I need to run, but thank you..." and she stumbled off with her boxes towards the entrance, leaving Thomas thoroughly embarrassed, and calling out before he could think,

"Annalise! Please wait," but she had already disappeared into the side door of the schoolhouse. He felt a complete fool. He resolved to locate her after the performance and offer to take her dress to the seamstress. What on earth had possessed him to call out using her first name? He should have used her surname, Miss Eddles! He thought her so pretty in the moonlight that instinct had taken over, and he used her Christian name. He hoped he did not look as foolish as he now felt!

Once inside the old barn that the villagers used as a schoolhouse, he found a seat toward the back, and quietly settled in for the performance. He was thrilled to see Sylvie in her first holiday performance, yet he could not shake off the humiliation he felt at knocking the teacher into the snow. The poor young woman! He hoped her ankle would be alright, and as he sat there with his conflicting thoughts, the makeshift stage curtains separated, and out came the children in all their costumes. Each child gave a lovely performance, but he had to admit that his Sylvie had done exceptionally well. Her singing voice was indeed just like an angel, and he fought back tears of pride. At the end of the performance, the lady he now knew as Annalise, came out to help the children take a bow. She announced that parents were to pick up their children at the side entrance one at a time to avoid chaos and confusion. Everyone clapped and cheered, and Miss Eddles led them off stage. Thomas was hoping that he could catch Annalise

Eddles when he went to gather his daughter. Then he could offer to have someone mend her skirt, and extend a more gentlemanly apology. He had noted that there was a small twig nestled in the woman's bun, as she came out onto the stage. She must have missed it in her hurry to assemble the kids and get the play started.

Thomas waited impatiently in line to collect Sylvie, and it felt as though his turn would never come. Finally, he heard a voice shout, "Daed!! Over here!" It was Sylvie standing over by the buggy! How on earth did she get out there before all the others?

"I'm over here, Sylvie! Wait there," and Thomas went to the buggy to take his daughter home. He regretted not being able to speak to the pretty Miss Eddles, but he wanted to celebrate with his daughter,

"What a marvelous song you got to sing! And all by yourself? What a surprise. I had no idea you were going to be singing a solo part!" He gave her a big congratulatory hug, and off they rode back to the farm.

After sharing a piece of pumpkin bread with his daughter, Thomas sat down to think over the events of the evening. He would have to seek out Miss Eddles tomorrow when he went into town to purchase feed. It would be Monday, and the children had been given a day off since the play had gone late. Perhaps the teacher would still be at the schoolhouse despite the children having the day off.

Monday morning came, and he watched lovingly as Sylvie went about her choring. He announced that it was the day for his monthly trip into town, so they said their goodbyes, and Sylvie promised to have a hearty supper ready upon his return. Thomas jumped in the buggy and proceeded towards his first stop; the schoolhouse. He felt butterflies in his stomach, and this unnerved him, because all he really intended to do was offer to mend the tear in her dress. It had been his fault after all. He pulled alongside the horse rail, fastened his buggy, and gave a feeble knock on the schoolhouse door. He heard light footsteps approaching, and Annalise Eddles opened the door. She seemed a bit shocked to see him, especially so early in the morning, but welcomed him in nonetheless,

"Good Morning, Thomas, is it?"

"Yes! Good of you to remember me," he stammered nervously," I just thought I would come by on the off chance that you'd be here, and offer to mend that awful rip that I caused in your lovely dress." He felt the words sounded all funny and awkward, as she smiled, and answered,

"Oh no, I stayed up last night and mended it myself. It was hardly anything to write home about, but thank you."

"Don't you have a family of your own to care for? I would hate to think I caused you extra chores so late at night," replied Thomas.

"No, I am unmarried, sir. It is just me and my rather fat cat, named Fred," Annalise replied with a chuckle. Thomas thought he noticed an all too familiar undercurrent of loneliness underneath the forced laughter. He wondered why this beautiful woman would feel anything but happiness.

"Again, I wish to extend my heartfelt apologies for yesterday. I know that my daughter, Sylvie, has much admiration for you. She speaks of you often..." and Thomas tried to think of something interesting to say, but all he could muster was,

"Are you busy, then, for Chrischdaag? Or do you and Fred have plans," he smiled and felt himself blush like a schoolboy. He could see the mixture of apprehension and the hint of a similar blush on her lovely cheeks,

"No, Fred and I were going to spend the day singing carols to each other," she laughed despite herself.

"Heavens, no! Please agree to join us at my farm. It will just be rather quiet with myself and Sylvie. You can even bring Fred along," he blurted.

"Well..." she thought aloud, "I suppose it would be a pleasant change of pace to have some company other than a cat wo can't sing very well. So, you think Sylvie would mind if I showed up at your front doorstep for Chrischdaag?"

"I think she would like the extra company, as would I, Miss Eddles."

"Please, call me Annalise," she said, and with that they parted ways agreeing that she should arrive bright and early on Chrischdaag morning. Thomas then realized that this was to be tomorrow. Uh oh! Would Sylvie be able to make enough dinner for three instead of two? Just in case, after he purchased the feed he had originally come for, her stopped off at the general store and ordered up a small, but very fine-looking turkey, some cakes and a pie, and chose a few gifts for Sylvie. He then returned home thinking to tell his daughter about their unexpected guest for tomorrow, but felt silly about it in the end. He figured it would just be a welcome surprise for Sylvie to see her teacher at the door in the morning.

That night, Sylvie worked long into the hours preparing the feast. She could see by the amount of work she had, that she bought enough food to feed an army, but she still had the peanut-brittle and divinity to make. She was so exhausted by the time the brittle was done, and she could barely keep awake. Sadly, she resigned herself to sleep, and figured one favorite was better than none, and moped off to bed. She even was too tired to change out of her day clothes, and fell instantly asleep covered in flour.

The next morning Sylvie awakened later than normal. She immediately got herself out of bed, because she knew the morning chores still had to be done, Chrischdaag or not! She changed into her work dress, and ran out to the kitchen to see if her father had already begun his day. There, much to her utter disbelief and shock, sat her daed and Miss Eddles sharing a cup of tea at the kitchen table! How could this be real, she thought!

"Daed! Miss Eddles! What are you doing here?" she cried, almost with tears in her eyes. That was the last thing she ever expected to see on Chrischdaag morning. It was infinitely better than all the gifts she had ever pined for, or all the sweets assembled on one table!

"Sylvie! Frehlicher Chrischdaag!" squealed her teacher, who was now standing up to greet an ecstatic little girl. It felt like all her prayers had been answered, and Gott had indeed seen it proper for her father and teacher to meet somehow. She cared little about how she was there, but was thrilled to pieces to see her lovely teacher at their home! It was just like a Chrischdaag miracle!

"Oh, my choring! Sorry, daed. I'll get moving right away, and then we can start breakfast!"

"It's alright, Sylvie!" cried Miss Eddles, "when I arrived this morning, we peeked in at you. You were sleeping so soundly that I went about and helped your daed with morning work. So, now all that's left for you to do is sit down and eat breakfast!"

"Yes, my dear daughter! And then afterwards, we will be blessed to have Annalise, I mean Miss Eddles, recite the story of the first Christmas from the family bible," Thomas beamed. And at that very moment, Sylvie burst into tears. Thomas and Annalise were both stunned at her reaction, taking it for disapproval and not the sheer happiness that it was. After all, how were they to know how hard Sylvie had tried to get them together. And to think that she had failed, and been so forlorn! She wondered how this has all come about,

"Oh! Daed! Miss Eddles! I wanted you to meet for such a long time now, and everything I tried always failed. Now to see you finally here on Chrischdaag! What a wonderful present! Will you be my new mamm now?" This proclamation made both Thomas and Annalise blush profusely, as neither one had realized how much Sylvie had wanted a mother. Annalise stared at the floor, not knowing what to say or how to react. She had wanted a family of her own for so long now, that Sylvie's reaction made her tear up. Thomas, however, noticed Annalise's reaction, and quickly came to her rescue, as he swooped her up, and began to dance her around the room as he sang a goofy rendition of Silent Night. Thomas knew that he was falling for the beautiful and caring Annalise, so he decided to play into his daughter's fantasy that he also wanted to see become a reality,

"Annalise. We have only just met, but I admit I feel a kindred spirit in you. Ever since we took that fall in the snow, something clicked inside me, and I have thought of you every minute since! Will you please consider becoming a part of our family? To be my wife, and a mother to Sylvie? We have lived far too long on our own," he pleaded against all reasonable and rational thought. Annalise stared at him open-mouthed, finally finding her voice,

"There is actually nothing I would rather do than just that!" she cried out, and everyone gathered in a weepy hug filled with happiness and joy.

As the day wore on, the threesome began to feel as natural as if they had always been destined to be together. It was time to exchange simple gifts, so Sylvie presented her father with the special peanut-brittle she had made. It was wrapped neatly in a kitchen cloth. His eyes widened and moistened to see his old favorite! How had she known, he wondered! The next to go was her father, and he presented her with a lovely handmade doll. It showed that he wanted her to enjoy being a child, and not worry so much about having to fulfill two roles. Sylvie hugged the doll, and named her Freddie, after Annalise's fluffy cat, who had already made himself at home in her lap! Finally, it was Annalise's turn to give her gifts. She presented the first to Sylvie, which was a gorgeous apron and matching bonnet,

"Sylvie, when your daed invited me over, all I could think of was how I would love nothing more than to pass on to you the gift my mamm made for me when I was your age. She died soon after, and I never had a girl of my own. I hope you like it" she cried, with yet more tears all around.

"Yes, I love it! Thank you so very much," and she ran to embrace the woman who was now to become her new mamm, "I love you so much, Miss Eddles!"

"Now, now. If I am to be your new mamm, you mustn't call me Miss Eddles anymore. Call me anything you feel comfortable with."

"Ok, then I shall call you mamm! I shall never forget my first mamm, but today I am given a new mamm," and Sylvie offered up a prayer of thanks to Gott for their good fortune. Just then, Annalise presented the last gift to Thomas. He graciously took her small box, and opened it only to find the most delicious looking divinity fudge he had seen in a very long while! Sylvie gasped in total surprise. How had she known? She couldn't have known. It turned out to be a very lucky guess on her part. And now Thomas stood up, and went to the trunk in the back room. He returned with a gift for Annalise. It was a very small box, dusty with years of remaining untouched. She opened the box only to discover a simple band of gold,

"Oh Thomas! How beautiful."

"That is my mother's wedding band that I have saved ever since her passing. Maddie was buried with her wedding band on, but I think she would approve of me offering it up to you. She has seen my loneliness these many years from up in Heaven, and now you are the blessing that we've all been praying for." She slid the ring onto her finger, and they sat down to the largest family meal any of them had ever seen.

"En frehlicher Chrischdaag un en hallich Nei yaahr!"

SWEET LONGINGS

STEPHANIE SWIFT

Rebecca Thompson put on her sunglasses and silently counted the steps it would take to reach the waiting limo from where she stood in the hotel lobby.

One...two...three...four...

Fifteen. Just fifteen steps and she would be in the safe confines of the backseat, away from the paparazzi peeking from behind the bushes near the entrance, ready to pounce on her as soon as she stepped outside.

Taking a deep breath, Rebecca secured her purse on her shoulder, pushed open the swinging door, and walked hurriedly to the waiting limo. Sam, her chauffeur, jumped from the vehicle as soon as he saw her approaching and hustled to the rear passenger door to open it for her. Unfortunately, in just a matter of seconds, the paparazzi had already swooped in.

"Miss Thompson! Miss Thompson! What can you tell TV Daily about your reprisal role in Lucky Girl?" one reporter asked.

"I'm sorry, Trudy, but you know I can't discuss the details of that right now. If you'll excuse me..." she responded.

Camera's flashed from every direction and Rebecca was momentarily blinded as she pushed her way through the ever-growing crowd.

Just seven more steps.

The reporters were always annoying but today they seemed positively relentless. She was used to a few of the regulars haunting her every step, but this was ridiculous. One particularly bold reporter attempted to stop her by grabbing her arm, but she jerked away from him and continued walking.

"Rebecca! Rebecca! Miss Thompson! What is your response to the rumor that your boyfriend has reconciled with his ex-wife?"

Rebecca stopped in her tracks and turned to face the reporter who asked the question. She laughed. Surely, he couldn't be serious. Her boyfriend, Colton, would never do such a thing. First of all, he despised his ex-wife. Secondly, he knew Rebecca would choke the life out of him if he even considered it.

"Where did you hear that?" she asked.

The others huddled around her with their microphones, cell phones, and various other recording devices. She lowered her shades and stared at the reporter who questioned her. His expression jumped back and forth between excitement over getting her attention and trepidation over what he may have just gotten himself into.

"*Where* did you hear that?" she repeated.

The young man put the microphone to his mouth.

"We received a tip from a credible source who saw your boyfriend and his ex-wife kissing in a corner booth at Shapiro's Restaurant last night. What is your response?"

Rebecca sucked in a breath. Unfortunately, she couldn't refute the statement because she honestly didn't know where Colton had been the previous night. After rehearsing scenes with some other Lucky Girl cast members on set, she had come home late and crashed.

Rebecca thought for a moment. Did she even speak to Colton yesterday?

No, this couldn't be true. It had to be another fabricated lie, like the numerous others she'd been subjected to during her acting career. Rebecca pushed the reporters out of her way and continued walking toward the waiting limo. There was only one way to find out for sure.

Sam opened the car door and Rebecca slipped inside and scooted to the opposite side of the limo, away from the glaring camera flashes and nosey journalists. Sam managed to fight his way through the throng of people, and when he took his place behind the steering wheel, Rebecca wasted no time in deciding her route.

"Take me to Colton's house."

* * * *

Rebecca bolted from the limo as soon as Sam brought it to a stop in front of Colton's mansion, not even bothering to wait for him to open the door for her. She paused for a moment and glanced around the property, noticing right away that Colton's new Jaguar and his antique Chevy Chevelle were parked inside the garage, which usually indicated he was home. Whether he was alone or not was a different matter altogether.

"Sam, please take the limo back to the hotel. This may take a while."

He looked apprehensively from Rebecca to Colton's house and back again.

"Are you sure, Miss Thompson? I don't mind waiting."

As much as she appreciated his concern, right now she had just one goal in mind.

"Please, Sam. I'll be fine. I'll call you when I get ready to leave."

He gave her a wistful look before getting back in the limo and making his way down the long and winding driveway. When he drove around a bend and out of sight, Rebecca approached the front door and pounded on it several times with her fist. For a moment, all was quiet. Then the door opened, but instead of his butler, it was Colton himself on the other side.

"Rebecca! W-what are you doing here? I thought you were supposed to be on set today," he stammered.

Rebecca glanced past him and into the enormous adjoining den, which appeared to be empty. She stepped forward and looked at him more closely. Upper lip twitching. Shifty eyes. Perspiration on his brow. Rebecca pushed him aside and walked in the house.

"Where is she?" she asked.

Colton tried to utter a reply, but it was so obvious he was lying. She knew him better than he knew himself, and he was one of the worst liar's she'd ever seen. Rebecca headed for the stairway leading to the second floor, but before she could take the first step, Colton jumped in front of her and blocked her path.

"What are you doing?"

She darted around him and raced up the stairs, taking them two at a time.

"I think I'm the one who should be asking YOU that question!" she yelled.

He caught up to her rather quickly, and each time he tried to stop her, she would push him out of the way. He switched between shouting obscenities to begging her to "be reasonable", which only added to her growing suspicion. When Rebecca arrived at Colton's bedroom, she yanked open the door before he had the chance to stop her.

She expected to find his ex-wife, Julia, lying in his bed, but she was nowhere to be seen. Rebecca quickly scanned the room, but it was empty. Colton stood nearby, panting from exertion, with his hands on his hips and never once meeting her gaze.

Something wasn't right.

Rebecca looked around the room again, and that's when she saw it – a tiny speck of blue peeking from underneath a pillow on the floor beside the bed. She walked over and kicked the pillow out of the way, unearthing a lacy blue bra lying beneath it. Her heart started racing and she could feel each pulse as it throbbed in her veins and made her head ache. Colton never said a word.

"Come out, Julia! I know you're here!" she screamed.

It was silent for a long time, but then Rebecca heard the closet door being opened slowly. The tension in the room was so thick you could cut it with a knife, and she didn't have to guess who was there. She knew. She felt the anger steadily building inside of her before she glanced toward the closet and saw Julia standing there, with nothing but a thin bed sheet covering her body.

She wanted to yell – to scream – to rip her hair out – and Colton's too. But what could he say that would make it all just a bad dream? This was really happening, and there was no way he would be able to discount something that was so blatantly obvious.

Rebecca left the room before she burst into tears. They could break her heart into a million tiny pieces, but she would die before she let them see her cry. Colton followed her as she ran for the stairway, and when he made the mistake of grabbing her from behind, she whirled around and slapped his left cheek...*hard*. The sound of it echoed through the empty corridor, and he clutched the bannister to keep from falling as he stumbled backward.

Rebecca continued down the stairway and went straight for the front door, grabbing a set of keys from atop a table in the foyer on her way out. There was no way she was going to wait for Sam or stoop to calling a taxi company, and she knew from her many times driving it that the keys belonged to Colton's Chevelle.

"Rebecca! What are you doing? STOP!"

She had to get out of there before she snapped. The air felt thick and burned her lungs as she ran toward the garage, with Colton not far behind. Rebecca jumped in the Chevelle and locked the doors. Seconds later, he was banging on the driver side window.

"Get out of my car, Rebecca!"

She glared at him as she put the keys in the ignition and roared the engine to life.

"I bought it for you, Colton, so technically it's MINE! Now move out of my way!"

She put the car in reverse and slammed on the accelerator, but unfortunately Colton jumped back before she had the chance to run over his toes. When she put the car in drive and started down the driveway, he tried to run after her, and as she watched his lone figure grow smaller and smaller in the rear-view mirror, Rebecca finally let the tears fall where they may.

* * * *

The New York city limit sign had long come and gone before Rebecca realized she'd left her purse in the limousine. The need to get as far away as possible had been too great to focus on anything else, and now as she coasted on fumes down an abandoned Pennsylvania dirt road, the severity of her situation was hard to ignore.

She knew she should have gone straight to her hotel, but she also knew that in no time at all Colton would show up, and she just couldn't face him again. So, she headed west, away from New York and the heartache and humiliation. She didn't have a cell phone, a paper map, or a GPS. She simply turned the wheels toward the open highway and never looked back.

When the fuel ran out and the engine began to sputter, Rebecca pulled over beside the road and stopped. *Now what?* The last gas station she'd passed had been several miles back – not that it mattered. She had no cash, no credit card, and the only change she could find inside the car was a measly 49 cents.

Rebecca leaned her head against the steering wheel. She didn't want to go back, but she'd spent the past five years with Colton, and she had no clue how to move forward either. The news had probably broken to all the major TV stations by now, and there would be no way to hide from it. All she really wanted was to disappear for a while.

She looked at the barren land surrounding her and she had to laugh when the realization hit her that she was off to a very good start. There was no way anyone would be able to find her in such a deserted area. The thought thrilled her but terrified her at the same time.

Rebecca got out of the car and leaned against the door. It was early afternoon, and there wasn't a vehicle or house as far as the eye could see. The hot August sun was unforgiving as she wiped the tiny beads of sweat from her brow and started walking. She didn't know where she was or how far she had to go to find help, but she did know she couldn't just sit inside a sweltering car and do nothing.

As Rebecca walked and walked for what felt like an eternity, she hummed her favorite songs, recited her Lucky Girl lines, and did whatever else she could think of to keep her mind occupied and not focus on the way her feet and back ached with every step. After rounding a curve, she spotted in the distance what resembled a horse pulling a buggy with two people sitting inside. Her heart began to pound with a mixture of hope and fear. What if they passed her by? What if they were serial killers?

She laughed. *Stop it, Rebecca. The heat is making you delirious.* As they got closer, she saw an elderly man at the reins and a woman sitting on the seat beside him who appeared to be about the same age. Both were dressed in Amish attire, and Rebecca expelled a sigh of relief. She moved over to the edge of the road and hoped they would stop and offer some assistance. When the man pulled up on the reins and brought the horse and buggy to a halt in front of her, she wondered briefly if they might recognize her from her acting roles. Did she want them to or not? Honestly, she couldn't decide.

"*Guder nammidaag*!"

Rebecca raised a brow. She had no idea what he said, but his smile was so big and warm, she immediately felt at ease.

"Hello," she replied. "Could you please tell me where I am? I'm afraid I might be lost."

They exchanged glances before the woman leaned forward to look at her more closely. Her brown eyes pierced right through her, leading Rebecca to take a cautious step backward.

"You're in Lancaster, Pennsylvania," she said. "Where are you from?"

Okay, so they didn't recognize her.

Rebecca tossed around her options. She could tell them, but then again that might lead to her returning to New York sooner than she wanted to. On the other hand, she could lie, but lying to an Amish person felt very sacrilegious and would possibly warrant a one-way ticket to Hell. As she struggled with the imaginary devil on her left shoulder and the angel on her right shoulder, the man and woman whispered to each other and continued with the worried glances.

"Dear, are you alright? You seem...disoriented," the woman said. "What is your name?"

Disoriented. That was it! She could pretend she'd lost her memory! If anything, it would help her bide her time until she could decide what she wanted to do, and since this was acting...well, it wouldn't *really* be lying.

"I...I don't know."

More glances.

"Do you have family here?" the man asked.

Rebecca thought about Colton to try and make herself cry, but that only made her angry, so instead she did what always worked when she needed to cry on demand – she thought about her first puppy, a sweet little Poodle named Amber, who died when she was fifteen years old. Within seconds, the tears were swelling in the corners of her eyes.

"I'm not sure," she replied. "I'm so sorry. I'll stop troubling you now."

She turned to walk away, but the woman scrambled down from the buggy to stop her. When she grasped her elbow, Rebecca turned to look at her with tears rolling down her cheeks. It had the effect she wanted, as the woman placed her hand over her heart and gave Rebecca the most pitiful look.

"*Neh*, dear. You're not troubling us at all. We would like to help you, if we can. My name is Hannah King, and this is my husband, Eli."

He tipped his hat to her, and she smiled at them both as she wiped the tears from her cheeks with the hem of her shirt sleeve.

"We live in a small community not far from here. We were just returning from Lancaster. It's getting late, but we can take you there tomorrow. Perhaps the sheriff will be able to help you."

Their willingness to aid a stranger took her by surprise. Being from New York, she wasn't used to such hospitality, and it filled her with guilt. Maybe this wasn't such a great idea.

"Thank you, but you don't have to do that. I'll walk to Lancaster..."

She tried to leave, but Hannah stopped her again.

"You will do no such thing. We have a spare bedroom, and you could probably use a hot meal and some rest."

She simply wouldn't be swayed, so there was no turning back. Hannah climbed up on the buggy and sat down beside Eli and then motioned for Rebecca to sit next to her. When they were situated, Eli made a strange whistling sound with his mouth and the horse went into an easy gallop.

She feared the ride to their home might be awkward and quiet, but she couldn't have been more wrong because Hannah talked nonstop. Rebecca learned their only child, Hope, had moved to a different Amish community in northern Pennsylvania with her husband and their four daughters. Hannah earned money making quilts and selling them in one of the Amish storefronts in Lancaster, and Eli worked as a blacksmith.

When they arrived at their home, Rebecca felt as if she'd learned their whole history, which made her feel even more uncomfortable, given the circumstances. They asked her questions, probably hoping to stir up a memory or two, but she played her part and acted aloof until they eventually stopped with the inquiry.

"Ah, Daniel! There you are!" Eli remarked. "Let's get these horses some extra grain before you leave. They've had a busy day, especially this one."

Rebecca leaned forward to see who he was talking to and she spotted a man approaching them from the opposite side. He took the reins from Eli before helping him and Hannah step down from the buggy. Unsure of what to do, Rebecca stayed put.

"Daniel, this is…well, it's a long story, but she's our guest and will be staying with us tonight."

He was very handsome and they appeared to be about the same age. He had on Amish attire, much like Eli was wearing. He was quite tall, with tanned skin and short brown hair. His face was cleanly shaven though, unlike Eli, who had a long gray beard.

"*Gut'n owed.* It's nice meeting you."

There it was again – more of that strange language she didn't understand. Daniel held up a hand to help her down, and when she placed her hand in his she noticed right away how warm his skin was, which sent an unexpected chill up her spine. Despite her wobbly knees, she managed to plant her feet firmly on the ground without stumbling over them and making a fool out of herself. While Daniel led the horse and buggy toward the barn on the far end of the property, she did her best not to stare after him.

"Now, let's get you settled in for the night," Miss Hannah said.

She smiled. Perhaps this wasn't such a bad plan after all.

* * * *

The sun was just starting to rise in the east as Daniel jumped from his wagon and walked hurriedly toward the King's front door. He was operating on little sleep, but he'd started out at first light so he could get there early and talk to their houseguest. Mr. Eli had shared very few details with him the night before, other than finding her walking the main road alone and that she appeared to have some type of amnesia. Even so, he had to admit he was very intrigued by this stranger who was, without a doubt, NOT from their community. When Miss Hannah opened the door, he did his best not to appear too enthusiastic.

"*Guder mariye*, Daniel. Come in."

He stepped inside the den and removed his hat before following her to the kitchen. Since he began working as Mr. Eli's assistant two years prior, he'd become accustomed to their usual morning ritual, which included eating breakfast with the couple before work commenced. Daniel's happy mood diminished when he walked in the kitchen and discovered Mr. Eli was the only other person in the room.

"*Guder mariye*," he announced.

The elderly gentleman nodded as Daniel took his place at the table, and he smiled at him, trying his best not to appear as downtrodden as he felt. When Miss Hannah put four heaping plates of scrambled eggs and bacon on the table, he felt his spirits lift again. She was still here! He grinned a bit more widely than he probably should have, and when the beautiful stranger entered the kitchen just moments later, he accidentally dropped his fork, causing it to clang loudly against the metal plate.

She was busy fiddling with the buttons on one of her sleeves, but when she looked up and saw him sitting there, she smiled.

"*Guder mariye*," Miss Hannah said. "I hope you slept well."

She gave Miss Hannah a curious look before sitting down on the opposite side of the table from him.

"*Guder mariye* means good morning," Daniel explained.

That seemed to help because she nodded as if she understood.

"I did sleep well. Thank you," she replied. "Miss Hannah, did you wash my clothes for me while I slept?"

She ran her fingers over the silky material of her shirt and gave Miss Hannah another strange look, as if the thought of her doing so surprised her for some reason.

"*Yah*, I did. They were quite dusty from your walk yesterday, so I washed them for you."

When she looked his way, Daniel noticed her eyes glistened with unshed tears. She cleared her throat and tried to inconspicuously wipe the teardrops from her eyes, but Daniel caught it, even if no one else did.

"That was so nice of you, Miss Hannah. Thank you."

When the couple reached out to join hands with them and pray over the meal, he wished he was sitting next to her so he could hold her hand. She glanced nervously at them before they prayed, but she gave them all a tentative smile before placing her hands in Miss Hannah and Mr. Eli's and bowing her head.

After Mr. Eli prayed, they talked about the day's work ahead of them while their guest sat quietly by and listened. He tried not to stare at her, but she was so beautiful it was difficult not to. Her raven-colored hair hung in waves that barely touched her shoulders, and her eyes were such a pale shade of blue they appeared almost gray. She seemed quite shy, which fascinated him even more. Who was this stranger and where did she come from? He wanted and needed to know.

When Miss Hannah mentioned taking her to Lancaster to speak to the sheriff, he saw an opportunity and took it.

"Miss Hannah, I can do that for you. Mr. Talbot said Mr. Eli's parcel should arrive in today's mail, so I can stop by the post office and check on that while I'm there. I mean, if it's okay with the two of you, of course."

He probably jumped at the chance a bit too abruptly, by the way the couple smiled at each other when he mentioned it. His glanced across the table as the heat began to rise to his cheeks, but thankfully their guest didn't object to his offer. After a brief discussion, Mr. Eli agreed to let him accompany her to Lancaster, and Daniel nodded, not trusting himself to speak for fear of embarrassing himself even further.

When they were finished with breakfast, she followed Daniel out the front door to his wagon. He planned to help her climb up the step, but she was much quicker than he was, and she was already seated and ready to go before he even had time to adjust his hat. After he took his place beside her, he couldn't help but notice how close she was. Their legs were almost touching, and even though he knew creating some space between them would be the gentlemanly thing to do, he just couldn't bring himself to move over. As he guided the horse and wagon toward the road and away from the King home, she glanced his way and smiled.

"Thank you for doing this," she said.

He looked forward, not trusting himself to stare at her for too long in case he accidentally veered them away from the road and into a ditch.

"You're welcome."

The clothes she wore reminded him of the plain women in Lancaster, who often wore pants and brightly colored blouses. The shirt she had on was made from a soft material he'd never seen before, and the color brought out the blue in her eyes. The wind picked up just then, and a few tendrils of her hair brushed against his cheek, making him inhale sharply as his heart thumped erratically.

"I noticed there's no electricity and no televisions or phones at the King's house."

He smiled. No, she certainly wasn't Amish.

"We don't believe in modern technology the way plain people do. It has a way of distracting us from living the way God intended."

She gave him a quizzical look.

"Plain people?"

He had to admit her innocence was quite endearing.

"People who aren't from the Amish faith and community."

She nodded, but she also grew quiet, which made him wonder if he'd said something wrong.

"Have you been able to recall any details from your life?" he asked.

She glanced sideways at him and shrugged her shoulders.

"No, not really. What about you? Do you live here? Are you married?"

Her sudden barrage of questions surprised him, and at first, he didn't know how to answer. She seemed curious, but he couldn't tell if her curiosity was genuine or if she was just trying to be nice.

"*Yah*, I live here, and I'm not married. I've worked as Mr. Eli's assistant for the past couple of years. He wants to retire from the blacksmithing trade soon, and he doesn't have a son or grandson to pass it on to, so he's training me to take over his business."

She became quiet again as she glanced around them at the rolling hillside, and he didn't interrupt her train of thought. He couldn't imagine being locked inside her mind, with no recollection of where she came from or even what her name might be. It had to be a very lonely and frightening thing to endure.

"I think it's nice. Your way of life, I mean," she said. "It's so peaceful here. I slept better last night than I have in a very long time."

Her comment confused him, since she supposedly couldn't remember anything about her life, but he didn't say anything. When they reached the end of the road and turned left onto the main road to Lancaster, she sat up straight and folded her hands in her lap. She wore a few pieces of jewelry, but there was no wedding band on her left hand, unlike some of the plain women he knew in Lancaster.

"I'm guessing you aren't married…"

Before he could finish his sentence, she turned abruptly in her seat to face him. He didn't look at her, but he could feel her eyes boring a hole straight through him.

"Why do you say that?" she asked.

He pulled back gently on the reins to make his horse stop walking. Her demeanor had completely changed, and he saw the way her eyes shimmered with tears. He felt like kicking himself, even though he had no clue what he'd done.

"I apologize. I didn't mean to pry. I just noticed you weren't wearing a ring on your left hand. I have plain friends who are married, and they all wear a gold band on this finger."

He touched the finger beside her pinkie on her left hand, and she looked at it longingly before a tear escaped and started rolling down her cheek. Before he had the chance to talk himself out of it, he gently wiped it away with his hand – a move that seemed to surprise her just as much as it did him.

"I'm so sorry. I never meant to make you cry."

Her eyes widened and she turned back around and looked straight ahead. She didn't say anything for a long time, and Daniel took that as a sign to leave her alone. He flicked the reins and the horse galloped forward, but he didn't say another word. Perhaps it was best to just let it go.

"I never stopped to consider it, but I suppose you're right," she said. "There isn't someone special in my life."

She said it so softly it was almost a whisper. He wanted to disagree with her and reiterate the fact that he didn't think she was *married* and not that she wasn't seeing someone, but he remained silent instead of risking tripping over his own tongue.

Neither of them spoke again throughout the rest of the trip, and when they arrived at the post office in Lancaster, he jumped down from the wagon and walked around to the other side to help her down, not that he expected her to accept his help. He did it simply because he'd been taught it was the right thing to do.

She surprised him by placing her hands on his shoulders, and he had no other choice but to grab her waist. She didn't let go right away when he set her down on the ground, and they stood so close he could feel her breath on his skin, but her expression was a difficult one to read. He did notice the way her beautiful blue eyes no longer sparkled the way they had earlier as they sat around the King's kitchen table, and that alone made him sad.

"I can come with you to talk to the sheriff, if you like."

She dropped her hands and stepped away from him. He pointed to the sheriff's office, which was four doors down from the post office, but she shook her head.

"No, thank you. I need to do this by myself."

He nodded.

"I'll meet you back here. Just take your time. No rush."

She smiled at him, but she didn't make a move, so he started for the post office to give her some space. Right before he stepped inside the building, he caught sight of her walking toward the sheriff's office. He knew he should feel happy over the possibility of her discovering where she belonged, but he also knew once that happened she would more than likely disappear from his life...and that dose of reality hurt a lot more than he expected it would.

* * * *

Rebecca sat on the edge of the bed and contemplated her next move. After tossing and turning most of the night, she removed the long flannel nightgown Miss Hannah gave her and put on her clothes. She could tell they'd been washed again, which made her feel even more guilty, if that was possible.

She couldn't get Daniel off her mind. He was so kind and such a gentleman, and there was no sense in denying it...she was falling for him. No, she wouldn't continue with this charade. She couldn't. Leaving him, however, was another heartache altogether.

She'd managed to sidetrack the sheriff's office as soon as she saw Daniel disappear into the post office, but it wasn't easy. The residents of Lancaster were particularly curious over her, and she couldn't move an inch without someone watching her every move. She worried that someone might recognize her, but no one approached her. (A fact that filled her with relief but also irritated her. Did these people NOT watch TV at all?)

Rebecca returned to the wagon seconds before Daniel did, and she concocted another story by telling him the sheriff promised to check the missing person's database frequently and stay in contact with her. He didn't question it, but she thought for certain she was busted when they passed a man on the way home who was hauling the Chevelle with a tow truck. Daniel turned and stared at it when they passed by, but if he noticed the New York license plate, he didn't mention it.

Rebecca hung her head in shame. This wasn't acting. She was deceiving good, honest people – simple as that. She picked up her shoes and tip-toed to the bedroom door, trying to step as lightly as she could to keep the wooden floor from creaking beneath her. They had no electricity, so thankfully there was no alarm system to alert the King's she was leaving. Once outside the house, she slipped on her shoes and took off in the direction of the main road that would lead her back to Lancaster.

She had no idea what time it was, but the sun was starting to rise. Before she could reach the main road, she caught sight of Daniel approaching in his wagon. She frantically searched for a place to hide, but there were no trees, no dwellings…just acres upon acres of open farmland in every direction. She moved to the side of the road as he drew near, but when he stopped in front of her, she couldn't bear to look at him. She knew without a shadow of a doubt that one look would give her away, and she just couldn't bring herself to hurt another person, especially not Daniel.

"You're leaving?"

His deep voice broke through the stillness and made her tremble. Rebecca turned away from him and walked faster toward the main road. She heard the wagon creak and then Daniel's feet hit the ground, but she refused to slow down.

"Wait!" he called.

No, she couldn't do this. She wanted revenge over Colton, but not like this. It wasn't worth it.

Daniel caught up to her and grabbed her arms from behind to make her stop. She thought he would let go right away once he had her still, but he didn't, and the heat from his hands seared through the thin material of her shirt and made her tremble once again.

"Please don't go," he whispered.

Rebecca closed her eyes and fought back tears. His breath was hot against the back of her neck, and she caught herself leaning into him, enjoying the warmth.

"I can't do this anymore. I've been lying to you, Daniel...to all of you. I never lost my memory. I was running away."

He dropped his hands and moved away from her. When she turned around to confront him, the look on his face was all it took to make the tears fall. His expression was a mixture of shock, sadness, and disbelief.

"My name is Rebecca Thompson, and I live in New York. I'm...I'm an actress."

He opened his mouth, but no words came out.

"I'm so sorry, Daniel," she continued, before he tried to stop her. "I discovered my boyfriend, Colton, was cheating on me, and I just took off. That car...the one you saw yesterday on our ride home...it was mine. I ran out of gas, and I didn't have any money, so I got out and walked. That's when the King's found me."

He removed his hat and ran his fingers through his hair as he paced back and forth. She waited for him to say something, but he was silent for so long she feared he never would.

"But why? Why would you lie? Why didn't you just tell Miss Hannah and Mr. Eli the truth from the start so they could help you get home?"

She wiped the tears from her face and crossed her arms over her chest.

"At first I wanted to disappear, but then I met you, and that changed things. I didn't want to leave."

He stopped pacing and looked at her. She closed the distance between them, and when he tried to back away, she grabbed his arms to keep him from doing so.

"We come from two very different worlds, Rebecca..."

She nodded solemnly before looking down and shuffling her feet in the dirt. She didn't know what to say, and she certainly couldn't argue with him. After all, he was right.

Before she could decide how to respond, he was pulling her close and claiming her mouth with his own. It all happened so suddenly, but it was a welcome surprise, and he didn't release her until she was left breathless and weak in his arms. Rebecca held on to him tightly to keep from falling.

"Does this mean you want me to stay?" she asked.

He took a step back, and when she saw the sadness in his eyes, she immediately wished she could take back the question.

"I'm afraid it's not that easy," he replied. "There are customs our people have been abiding by for many years..."

Rebecca nodded and held up a hand to keep him from saying anything further.

"It's okay, Daniel. I understand."

He gently brushed his fingertips against her cheek and smiled.

"I didn't say it was impossible."

Rebecca's spirits soared. Perhaps there was hope for them after all. Still, she was afraid to move, to breathe…to break the spell that might make it all come crashing down around her.

"You've got to tell the truth, Rebecca. We can't try and build something together based on a lie. It won't work."

She nodded.

"I know, and you're right."

He glanced toward the sun that was now peeking over the horizon. She wondered for a moment if Miss Hannah and Mr. Eli were awake, and if they had noticed she was gone or that Daniel was late for work. Her heart ached for so many different reasons – partly from guilt, but most of all from wanting something so badly that might never happen.

"What about New York, your career…and your boyfriend?"

She sighed.

"The only thing left for me in New York is my job, and I'm not even sure I want that anymore. I do know that I'm through with Colton. That should have ended a long time ago."

Rebecca placed a hand against his chest before standing on her tiptoes so she could kiss him again. Her heart raced when he pulled her into his embrace instead of pushing her away, like she feared he would. It felt wonderful, but most importantly, it felt *right*.

"Daniel, I don't have all the answers. This is new to me too, but I promise you I want this to work, and I'm ready to do whatever it takes to make that happen."

Her answer seemed to satisfy him, and he smiled as he grabbed her hand and began pulling her toward the wagon.

"Okay, then the first thing you need to do is tell Miss Hannah and Mr. Eli the truth. They are the closest thing I have to a family, and I know they will do whatever they can to help us."

Rebecca groaned as he helped her into the wagon. It wouldn't be easy, but as she watched Daniel sprint around the wagon and take his place on the seat beside her – grinning the whole time – she knew without a doubt that it would be worth it in the end.

"We'll get through this...together," he said.

Rebecca huddled close to his body and smiled.

Together – what a beautiful place to start.

www.ingramcontent.com/pod-product-compliance
Lightning Source LLC
Chambersburg PA
CBHW021214160726
47994CB00001B/469